# CHURCHMEN'S
## GRAVEYARD

**Kator Hule-Ingya**

Copyright ©Kator Hule-Ingya, 2018



**ISBN:** 978-978-964-627-2
First Published by Old Press

**OLD PRESS**
Imprint of PEA & Associates
No. 34, Ankpa Road, Makurdi, Benue State.
Email: konkofibooks@gmail.com
Phone: +2348189844250, +2348059955218

**Abuja Office:**
ANA Secretariat

# PRAISES FOR THE BOOK

*...an interesting and touching story... very educative and instructive too.*
**Regina Achie Nege** – Freelance Editor


*...a good account of what happens in our institutions of higher learning.*
**Patience Onekutu**, PhD – University of Agriculture, Makurdi


*...vividly and fantastically narrated, highly intriguing and totally captivating.*
**Baroness Vivienne Vanger** (1982 – 2016)
Author of *Your Character & Destiny.*


*...brisk and brave; relevant to our times.*
**Unoma Nguemo Azuah**
Professor of Creative Writing
*Illinois Institute of Art*, Chicago, IL


*A simple, playful yet painful realistic story of the moral struggles of today's youth.*
**Sam Abah**, PhD.  Lead Mentor, Grassroot Africa


***Kator Hule-Ingya*** *has done a great job in this book,* ***"Churchmen's Graveyard".*** *Written in a lucid and flowing language, the work critically and meticulously exposes and reflects with the exactitude of a Jewish Prophet... A masterpiece written by an insider; you will miss this succulence if you depend on second hand information about the content of this novel.*
**Revd. Fr. Solomon Ukeyima**
Parish Priest, St. Augustine Parish, Demekpe, Makurdi

*I believe in your strength; it is your most worthy asset*
*And your weakness is not for always*
*You will surely become your good dreams*
*Do not give up on yourself*

**'Dance of a Madman'**, in: *Sunshine, This Is Our Day!*

**...'Kator Hule-Ingya, 2017.**

# DEDICATION

When the manuscript of this book was first drafted over eleven years ago in my 100 Level at the university, I felt highly to dedicate it to people who were very dear to my heart. Today too, my love for them remains immeasurable. They are:

Wase Ezekiel Terwase (1991-2006); last of my mother's children, so kind-hearted and so deep-loving. "Man-Mountain", we truly miss you. And, I wish you lived to see our father get his PhD.

Aker Iorpenda (1979-2005); a schoolmate turned friend and then brother. You were such a promising chap! Now, so much missed.
Well, I had to use your name for the protagonist in this story to immortalize you. I hope it's ok?

Andrew Hule Ingya (1914-2003); My very inspiring grandpa! You were a burner from where I tapped my light: This light I will always let to shine, even if I should stand alone.

And to:

His Royal Majesty, Begha u Tiv Orchivirigh Professor James I. Ayatse, Tor Tiv the IV; former Vice-Chancellor of the Federal University of Agriculture Makurdi, Nigeria; former Vice-Chancellor Federal University Dutsin-ma, Katsina State, Nigeria – for your brave fight against campus cultism at the Federal University of Agriculture Makurdi during my studentship.

His Excellency Rotimi Amaechi; Nigeria's Minister for Transport; former Governor of Rivers State – for his strong belief in the Nigerian literature – for his concerted efforts as a state governor to ensure that Nigerian writers carved words out with renewed/ fabulous dexterity.

I am only very proud of you all!

# FOREWORD

Kator Hule-Ingya's book, *Churchmen's Graveyard* simply passes as a touching, educative and indeed and instructive story which I must confess will remain an invaluable tool to the youths in our schools of higher learning for a long time. This well thought out and well written story stands in a class of its own. And I believe that although there are a number of writers making a difference in this country. The arrival of *Churchmen's Graveyard* by Kator Hule-Ingya is an announcement of the marriage of Environmental Engineering and a vivid literacy enterprise.

This book is an attempt to document for posterity a detailed investigation of the younger generation in campuses. The depth of content and social responsibility makes cross-generational connect in relation to harrowing experiences of unsuspecting undergraduates with cult groups on campuses and unavoidably impacts the reader. For sure, this book has to be a MUST READ for all youths, especially those on campus. The book will not only challenge you but will inspire you and definitely serve as one of the key books to awaken all parents in Nigeria, reminding them that they are in the race of life for their children in institutions of higher learning.

I would like to make it a commandment that every parent must read this book. If you do, you will never again be the same after you take the opportunity to absorb this fantastic book. Most parents and children when growing up dream of living with husbands, wives, beautiful homes and perfect children but what happens when life doesn't turn out the way they had hoped? Parents wonder why and what went wrong in the lives of their children. Kator brings this powerful message to all parents that when it comes to our collective desires, hopes and dreams for the generation right next door, there is no detail that is too miniscule or minutely insignificant for us.

The book captures the meteoric rise of cult activities and its attendant consequences on us. It is not my goal to sit in judgement of Kator's words, methods or doctrine in writing this book. Similarly, it is not my goal to roundly justify or validate many moves he has made in the book. Rather, it is my intention to examine Aondoakaa's triumphs as well as his trails that we might better understand how he survives the gruesome experiences and how he emerges as the best graduating student in his department.

This book will make an eternal difference in the lives of many in obscurity, as it honors and encourages them in their calls. God will continue to honor the tireless labor of our faithful men and woman who serve him across Nigeria in fighting cults in our institutions of higher learning. To them, I hope this book says, God sees what you are doing and he will honor your faithfulness as well.

Churchmen's Graveyard, written from the depths of Kator's heart will help youths in schools to turn past mistakes into triumphs. Don't let it die in your hands. Pass it on.

Those who are lost can indeed be found. Come take a closer look!

**Bishop Dr. Mike Judah Angou**
PFN Benue State Chairman

## TO MAMA ON MY CONVOCATION DAY

Mama, I still see Mother Mary and Child Jesus in the moon these days. I see them each time the moon is full, when I look up in the sky at night. Mother Mary always holds Child Jesus in her arms. They are peaceful and loving. This reminds me of my own childhood, how much love you watered on me.

Even now, as my convocation ceremony at the university is about to start, I can see Mother Mary and Child Jesus. But now, they are only blurry images in a blank mind! My mind is blank.

Mama, the time here now is 9:42. It is morning. A breezy and dry Saturday. And maybe, it is a special day. Maybe the convocation makes this day special.

You would probably wonder what a convocation ceremony is. I will tell you. But even though you may not wonder Mama, I will still tell. It is a kind of ritual with mysterious significance. Here, today, there will be certification or the certifying of academic performance and moral uprightness. It will be a verbal certification, more or less; something like when a physician does take an ailing person to the theatre, picks out the ailment and thereafter says to the patient, "You are now well. You can go home". Somehow, those words suddenly pump confidence in that patient. They become a healing balm.

So also, the university threats granduands; at the convocation ceremony, the graduands are professed fit in character and learning. A convocation is in fact a confidence licensing ritual.

Oh Mama, did you also probably wonder what a theatre is? At best, I can say, it's like a kitchen where a physician works all manner of his things. I hope you can make out what I mean. Well, this is probably the much I can say. Otherwise, I would bother you with too much tall grammar.

Right now, Mama, my joy has slumped. Sad memories have filled my mind. Do you wonder why I am seeing Mother Mary and Child Jesus in my mind on this convocation day? It is because my world is now under shattered stars. I think I am lost!

Very well, the *Oga* of the convocation ceremony is here! I have a pamphlet in my hand. It was given to me earlier by a girl with a name tag, "Usher". On it is written "Programme of Events". As I open the Programme of Events, I can see Oga's name, Chief Okafor Eze, clearly written under his portrait photograph. Okafor is an Ibo chief; but hence, I will regard him as he deems, the Chancellor.

In fact, there is a crowd here, a real rowdy crowd. It is perhaps the police band that is playing drums and blowing the bugle that has raised the noise to a shrill tempo.

Please Mama, try to understand – these are just the preliminaries of the convocation ritual.

There are cameramen here too. They have these big cameras with long lenses. They go around squatting here and there to capture the Very Important People's (VIP)'s faces. By tomorrow or so, one would see those pictures populating dailies and weeklies, in newspapers so that the common man on the street can read the great happenings around the VIPs. But sometimes, the common man is captured in the papers also, especially when there is the need to send his pitiable face abroad so as to solicit for help from the West. 'These are poor victims of HIV and AIDS in Africa. Send us help!' The cry goes.

'Every poor person in Africa has AIDS. Why are the black monkeys like that?' The *Oyibo* people in the West would wonder. Mama, you may not understand what I mean, I am sure.

Alright, the *Crème da la crème* are here. And you can't believe who I have spotted in this crowd. Mama, it's Anita! Anita! Oh, forgive my surprise. I was hopeful to see her here today anyways. And, only now do I remember, you do not even know her. Actually, we met earlier today when she arrived at the convocation ground. She told me that she is already married. She and her husband are living in the city of Lagos. I am happy for her... I am. 'How is your mother?' I asked her. 'Mummy passed on earlier this year', Anita replied, her face sagged briefly before she lifted her eyes and added. 'Her drink was poisoned in one of the campaign rallies'. I jerked with a punch of shock, then made it obvious to her that it was sad to hear that. 'God rest her soul in peace', I said shaking my head.

'Your Mummy was such a solid woman', I added.

Politicians have a game of their own. And, it is difficult to explain – just as it is difficult to explain why a goat, though it eats grass like a horse, remains just its dwarfish self. Anita's mummy was a politician.

Very well. I have just adjusted my necktie. It's almost choking me.

I must be honest with myself; I have not followed things here at the convocation as I should, except now that a man of stunted height has climbed the podium and breathed heavily into the microphone. 'Ladies and Zentru-men, flease, let us welrcome za frocession of za Senate.' It is difficult to tell whether this man is speaking English or Hausa, even Swahili!

Members of the University senate are matching towards the convocation tent in their regalia from the left wing of the tent. This is why we are all getting up to our feet. One can hear the seats cracking under the loss of weight. This moment appears to be important.

It's 10:07a.m. I flash a glance at my watch.

Two things will take place at this prestigious ritual, Mama. First, the granduands will be admitted to the various degrees; degrees will be conferred and prizes awarded. This is where I shall benefit. The second part is something I don't quite understand fully myself; it appears that the university would be selling degrees to three state governors and the Governor of the Central Bank of Nigeria. And why not?

The other time such a ritual was held here, one former state governor was sold a doctorate. As the former governor left the convocation ground, he narrowly escaped a team from the Economic and Financial Crimes Commission (EFCC) who were waiting to pick him up at the school gate. It was rumoured that the man had embezzled months' salaries of pensioners in his state. Mama, do you know what the former governor said afterwards? 'My political demons are after me to stop me from going to The Senate', his very words. But a newspaper insisted he had used the pensioners' money to come make the purchase.

The universities carry out such transactions not out of greed but as a little source to boost infrastructure. It would be completely wrong to place the act in the same box with that of the Almajiris who go begging from street to street in Northern Nigeria to ensure survival.

There is need to improve these infrastructures at the universities, no matter what. And, this is the truth! Who is talking about university autonomy? What's that! University autonomy is like telling the fowl that since its *nyarsh* is closer to the ground, it should use the *nyarsh* to pick grains.

Lecturers are employees, not business owners. The mindset of an employee is different, completely different, from that of a business owner. And it is only futile trying to fit the two into the same box.

What therefore is the right thing to do? A good General carves out the war plan and lets his lieutenants and soldiers fit in. That's how to win a war! Universities should be managed in a like manner.

Mama, I am only talking to myself. These blurry images stalked in my mind have intensely distorted my thought.

'Ladies and Zentru-men, fleese, you may resume your seats. Zank you.' The man says, and we do as he requests.

I take my handkerchief from my trousers pocket and clean sweat off my face. It seems I am bored with this function already. I slip the handkerchief back into the pocket and clear my throat.

Mama, there is a man sitting there in the senate section whom I should talk to you about. His name is Professor Uzu. This man gave a classmate of mine a carryover in his course in our final year. But that is not what I intend to say. Professor Uzu is a man of his own kind, almost a comedian. I must say.

Uzu's story is weighty to the mouth – else how would it be heard in the ear that the juju priest impregnated the mad woman – and I would be held responsible for telling the dirty secret. But that is what happened. Professsor Uzu fought with a colleague in a senate meeting. The news was everywhere on campus!

Uzu had been known to be full of himself in senate meetings. Each time he stood to address an issue in a senate meeting, he reminded the senate that he is Western trained – more properly prepared – and not half baked like those professors from local mushroom universities. Uzu would expect the senate to stand still until he had walked on heads. It was when the man started this usual wrecking in one of the senate meetings that the colleague stood and spoke the mind of all: That people who went to wash plates in *Oyibo* countries should be careful to identify themselves with the distinguished title. Uzu did not take the words kindly.

What followed, I am sure you can tell.

I can make out few more faces there, where the senate sits.

There is Processor Lar, the dean of my faculty. This is another *Oyibo* trained professor. But he doesn't carry it on his head, except for his distinguished raise-left-shoulder-drop-right-shoulder gait.

There comes the Chancellor's procession! And the Distinguished Chancellor himself is leading the long line of personalities. That's the line with the Registrar, two of our dear state governors, a Minister of the Federal Republic, and the Vice Chancellor.

'Distinguished ladies and zentrumen, let us rise for za National Anzem.' The man's eyes rest on the police band until they begin to play the hymn of allegiance. There is a lot of shuffling of feet on the floor as we all get to our feet - accompanied as usual by seats cracking nosily under the loss of weight.

The anthem is played and the representative of the president who is called "The Visitor" takes his seat. And then, we too do same.

Mama, the ritual is becoming a bit more engaging.

'Distinguished ladies and zentrumen, it's my fleasure to handz over za mic to za Registrar of Kwancil for conducting zis ceremoney,' the voice comes. 'Mister Registrar, Sir.'

Mr. Registrar rises and goes to the podium. He doffs his cap when he approaches the podium stand.

Now, he taps on the mic with his finger twice to ensure it is functional and then speaks. And as if his sight is suddenly inadequate, the man readjusts his spectacles, pulling the frame down the ridge of his nose so that he can look at the pamphlet on the podium-stand from over the spectacles. 'Th-e-eh Vi-si-tor,' the man salutes. He regards few more offices, coughs, apologizes, lifts his eyes briefly, returns to the pamphlet and continues to speak into the mic until he delivers what appears to be a welcome speech or something similar. He invites the Chancellor. And then, retreats.

There is absolute silence everywhere now; except for a few feet shuffling on the floor and a cautious cough once coming thinly through the air.

The mood is a happy one for most people here.

The Chancellor stands and goes to the podium stand. At the podium, he doffs his cap and speaks in a solemn voice. The man, vested with appropriate authority, declares the ritual open. When he ends the declaration, he looks at the crowd just for a while and says 'Thank you and I hope we will all have a great convocation ceremony.' He doffs his cap again and withdraws from the podium to his seat. He is given a resounding ovation.

My eyes rest on Anita again but it's just an idle going-around of the eye. Nothing particular to it. The sight is soon lost to the Vice Chancellor as he approaches the podium stand.

Mr. Vice Chancellor is a man I regard as one gentleman of honour. He has his feet on the rocks of time for his fierce fight with cultism in the university. A fearless man he is. Today, although such a tall man, he appears a little hideous in his academic regalia. But his voice comes loud and clear through the sound system. He doesn't talk for long like one thought he would. He simply talks about the background of the university. How the university started. Then he says something like: The university has challenges here and there, we need this and that, and look forward to kind-spirited individuals and organizations to come to our aid. Then, thank you very much and thank you indeed all. And have safe journeys afterwards.

The Vice Chancellor retreats to his seat. Ovations follow as appropriate.

The Registrar comes again to the podium stand. A circled-face man, his spectacles appears to sit better when pulled down the ridge of his solid nose. Mr. Registrar doffs his cap and breathes a womanish voice into the microphone as he slides his spectacles down his nose-ridge again. 'Chancellor Sir,' he says, 'the persons who will be presented by the Deans of Faculties have fulfilled the requirements of the regulations of the University of IBRU, and have been found worthy both in character and in learning to be admitted to the Bachelor's Degrees of their respective faculties. I therefore invite the Deans of the Faculties to present their grandaunds.'

The registrar begins to call the names of Deans of Faculties. The crowd is cheering vivaciously.

Soon, the Registrar invites Professor Lar, the Dean of my faculty, to present his grandaunds. Professor Lar goes to the podium. Now he gets to the stand and doffs his cap. 'May all the granduands of Religion and Philosophy rise, and remain standing.' His speaking-through-the-nose accent is always unmistakably *Oyibo* trained. I smile as the man throws his voice into the microphone.

We have risen from our seats, about two hundred grandaunds. Almost all of us are in a blue academic garment which is embroidered with gold stripes from collar to the shoulders.

This moment is particularly very crucial, Mama.

'Chancellor Sir,' Lar continues, 'In the name of the Faculty of Religion and Philosophy, and by the Authority of Senate, I present to you By-elm Ondokaa and two hundred and four others whose names appear on this list; those here present and those unavoidably absent to whom I stand proxy, who have been found worthy both in character and in learning to be admitted to the degree of Bachelor of Arts of the University of IBRU.' Applauses follow. I am not applauding, however.

By-elm Ondokaa? Professor, is it 'By-elm' that you called or 'Byem?' And then you got my first name wrong too! It is A-on-do-a-kaa.

Not Ondokaa! Don't be too English with my names. Kpash!

I rise. So does the rest of my course mates. Seats cracking, feet dragging noisily here and there. A cameraman squatting beside me hurries to our front. When we are all standing, the eyes of my mind run home to St. Winifred in Akan behind the new building which Father Gregory has started. The eyes stop on a grave. It's beside the grave of Vincent, the seminarian. Mama, here I see you again!

I hiss. My head slumps. And, immediately, my nose begins to sweet.

# Planting Guinea-Corn Seeds

### St. Winifred, Akan 

Mama, Eliza our neighbour, and I sat in front of our hut on a wooden bench one evening in St. Winifred, Akan. The sun had sunk and a crescent moon partially lit the dark skies. Father Gregory, the Catholic Priest at St. Winifred's Parish whom we were living with, had retired to his room. Mama brought a calabash half-filled with melon-seeds and began hulling them with Eliza. She had prepared roasted yam for me with palm oil and onion sauce. It was our usual for supper. I eagerly ate my share with relish.

Mama would later prepare soup with the melon seeds. She would grind the hulled seeds on a millstone and roll the paste into sizeable balls to make very tasty soup. She would cook the balls in a mixture of boiling water, palm-oil, ground pepper, salt, dry-fish and *nune.* Minutes later, Mama's soup would be ready.

Eliza who sat inches away from Mama stretched and whispered something into her ear. She then laughed. Mama laughed too. Mama then turned to me and said, 'Don't drink too much water Aondoakaa, the evening is far gone. If you empty your bladder on the bed this night, I will break your head.'

I lowered the cup of water I was drinking to the ground.

'Perhaps you should get up and go to bed now,' Mama continued.

'Mama, I am not feeling sleepy yet,' I pleaded.

'Get up and go to bed, I say. By the way, you will have to wake up early tomorrow so I will take you to school for enrolment. Now get up at once before I break your head.'

I stood as Mama had instructed. Nevertheless, I dreaded the loneliness of the hut, preferring to hang around and listen to their banter. I wished I retired to the hut with Mama later. Worse still, a dog barking faintly in the distance added to my trepidation. Eliza's husband had once told me that dogs have eyes for evil; that when they barked so aggressively at night, evil was hovering in the air. This heightened my fears.

'Aondoakaa, I say go to bed!' Mama said firmly as I stood there reluctantly. 'I will not ask you a third time, you rude boy! Do you hear me?'

'Yes, Mama,' I answered then started moodily for the hut, trembling as I went.

'A-o-n-do-akaa!' Mama called, 'Return and take this plate and cup along with you.'

I returned and picked the cup then headed for the hut again.

Eliza laughed. 'He is scared of being alone in the dark', she told Mama.

'Don't forget to pray before you sleep,' Mama said as I approached the door and gave it a slight push. I feared that some evil and horrible creature might be lurking behind the door, waiting to grab me.

'Enter inside that room at once and don't let mosquitoes in!' Mama shouted. I jerked with fear; dropping the metallic plate. The plate made a loud noise as it hit the floor. 'Be careful with the plate,' Mama yelled.

When I picked the plate, I noticed my left nostril was wet. I stuck a finger in and brought out something I was sure was blood. I was too scared to go back to Mama and inform her I was bleeding. Instead, I pushed the door at once, ran into the hut and shut the door.

Inside the room, a hurricane lamp burnt with a dim yellow light emitting tiny twirls of smoke. I dropped the plate and cup beside the lamp. We had no kitchen then. So, Mama would keep all her cooking utensils in the room. She cooked outside the hut at the hearth where she had arranged three stones to support pots in the open air.

A little mouse hurried across the room. It ran into a crypt on the floor at the foot of the mud wall. I trembled. With my heart still thumping, I knelt by the bed and said the "Hail Mary".

My left nostril itched with blood. Soon, the blood was trickling slowly down to my lips. I held the ear of my shirt and wiped the nostril thoroughly. Removing my slippers, I climbed into bed. The horrible creature was certainly creeping into the room. My heart pulsed. But it was not quite long before I slept.

In my sleep, I dreamt that Eliza gave birth to rompers. The rompers became a little scrawny puppy. This puppy sat at our door. It was playing with a sucked orange hull. The puppy was staring at me. I threw a stone at it. It began to laugh like an elderly woman. Instantly, it turned to a monster. The monster had an elephant's ears. It also had a mouse's whiskers, and a tooth that was the size of four large tubers of yam. It waddled towards me like a duckling. I began to run, heading to the market where I would meet Mama. I was panting heavily.

Luckily, I met Mama on her way. She was returning from the farm with a bundle of firewood on her head.

'Aondoakaa, stop at once'! Mama said. I halted.

'Why are you running madly like a fowl whose head is wringed?' she sought.

Looking around, the monster was no longer there. 'I want to go and wee-wee,' I said sheepishly.

'Go and wee-wee at the back of our hut,' Mama instructed. I nodded quietly, turned to the back of the hut. There, I peeled off my pants and began to urinate.

When I woke from sleep, I realized it was on the bed I was urinating so calmly! Mama was surely going "kill" me! The no-nonsense woman she was, if Mama would find out I urinated on the bed again, she would teach me a lesson I would never forget.

Mama and I shared a bed. I turned quickly and checked to see if Mama was in bed. She was not. It was already morning. She was up and out of the room. Rays of light filtered into the hut through the open door.

The lantern had been put out. It was still there by the door. Beside the lantern, Mama placed the wooden bench she had sat on the previous night against the mud wall of the hut.

I heard Mama's footsteps approach the hut, then she pushed the door. I quickly shut my eyes, pretended I was still sleeping. She walked into the room and picked a plate from the basket. My heart began to thump loudly. I feared she would come to the bed. Then, she would perceive the urine. But she did not. She was certainly cooking some food. She had no time for me yet. I heard the sound as she ran water into a pot.

Eliza's voice came through the door, 'Mama Aondoakaa, help me with table salt'. She requested.

Mama fetched a handful of table salt and left to meet Eliza. It occurred to me that I should jump up and change my pants. But just then, Mama's voice came from outside the hut 'Aondoakaa! Aondoakaa!! Get out of bed and come here!'

I stretched and feigned a yawn as if Mama was still there and could see me. I sat up. The stench of urine hit my nostrils as I slipped out of bed, cowering in shame.

'Aondoakaa! Aondoakaa!! Get out at once. Come and brush your teeth!'

'Yes Mama,' I said, quickly pulling off my stinking wet shorts. I put on a fresh dry pair before leaving the room. When I got outside the hut, I saw Mama standing beside the hearth. She was cooking.

'Mama, *u nder vee*?' I greeted, bowing respectfully.

'Come and brush your teeth!'

'Yes, Mama.' I stuttered. I was really scared Mama would notice I had urinated on the bed. Just as I thought, when I got close to her she asked, 'Did you urinate on the bed again?'

My breath ceased. I shook my head quietly. She stared for a while and then began brushing my teeth. Even though I was six years old, sometimes, Mama delighted in brushing my teeth. She would even bath me; especially when it was a Sunday, when we were preparing for church. That day, I wished she would allow me to myself.

'Come closer. And, stop wasting my time!'

I edged forward reluctantly. Mama spotted blood stains on my shirt. 'Is this blood on your shirt?' She enquired.

I nodded.

'Why is there blood on your shirt?'

'My nose bled last night.'

She stared sternly at me for a while as if to say I needed to always keep her informed if anything happened to me. Instead she said, 'Open your mouth, and stop wasting my time!'

I opened my mouth and positioned my teeth. Bending over my shoulders, Mama asked again why I was smelling of urine. 'You have urinated on the bed again, you foolish boy!'

I was quiet.

'I am asking, did you urinate on the bed? Answer me!'

But I only jerked with fear and shook my head.

'Come closer, let me take your bath', Mama said as she bent to scoop with the small bowl from the pail of water. Just then, Eliza called out from her kitchen. 'Mama Aondoakaa, can you help me with some palm oil?' She asked. It was the woman's peculiar habit to always request for one thing or the other from my mother. Mama had got used to it. She was never tired of helping out, no matter how many times Eliza had asked. Sometimes, it was the last bit of things Mama had. She would still give happily.

Eliza came over to meet us.

'Let me bathe the boy while you get the oil for me,' she offered.

Mama obliged. She left at once to our hut.

Eliza fetched a bowl of water, lifted it over my head and poured. I shut my eyes and caught my breath, rubbing water off my stomach as it ran down.

'Still! Stand still.' Eliza said.

I struggled to hold my breath.

'Still!'

Eliza picked a piece of blacksoap. She crushed it onto a sponge made from *toho-gile* grass. The soap smelt awful, like wet ash. As she ran the sponge on my face, my chest, my hands and then my belly, I wobbled continuously. Eliza was moving the sponge down my crotch. She ran it over my my *ajuju*. I felt tickled.

'Hie, hie,' I laughed.

'You, stand still!' Eliza cautioned, and then she picked my *ajuju* with her fingers. She caressed it lightly. It tickled so much. 'This is too big for a boy,' she said. Then between something that appeared to be chuckles, she added, 'Your *ajuju* is as big as a tuber of yam!' I smiled too, in a bit of shame, wishing she stopped the caressing. Fortunately for me, Mama emerged from the hut with palm oil in a bowl. When Eliza saw Mama coming, she withdrew her hand quickly and sank it in the bucket of water.

Even only still a child, I noticed that there was something strange about Eliza, something empty and frictional. Sometimes, she would keep laughing to herself. At such times, she would also laugh at almost everything. There was something else about the woman; everything that visited her mind would never sit there. It would run out quickly through her mouth. Her husband had once told Mama that the woman had a leaking mouth. But Mama said Eliza was one free spirit that was only full of her life.

Presently, Eliza rinsed her hands. She wiped them on her wrapper. Gratefully, she collected the bowl from Mama and left.

'Be still!' Mama cautioned. She poured water over my body.

'We will get to the school late if you don't stop wasting my time,' she cautioned as I held my breath.

'Have you defecated this morning?' Mama asked; the sponge was running on my crotch again. 'Hie, hie, Mama, its tickling…'

'Have you defecated this morning?' She asked again. I shook my head. She poured water over me once more to wash the fume. 'Run to the back of our hut and defecate. Don't defecate by the roadside. Enter inside the bush. Go towards those banana plants. Hurry!'

I skipped to the back of the hut towards a small cluster of banana plants and heaped a mound of excreta under one of the plants. Afterwards, I ran back. When I got back and stood before Mama, a housefly perched on my buttocks. Mama drove it away with her hand. The insect buzzed and returned.

'You must wash your hands each time you defecate,' Mama said.

Mama was soon through with bathing me. She dropped the bowl into the empty bucket and wrapped a piece of her wrapper round me. She held me by the hand and led me into the hut where she began to dress me up. Mama's life was so easy that I did not realize that my clothes were cheap. In fact, I could not tell we were very poor. She clothed our poverty with love.

But Mama's love never came with a kiss on my forehead; like white mothers dish kisses to their children in movies. Neither did it come in clear words of 'I love you Son' as some rich Nigerians say to their boys. It came with an effort to give me all life had deprived her of, all that she could afford. Sometimes it came as frustration also. Like the story of Joseph in the Bible which Mama would later tell me, whose father gave him a coat of many colours, Mama's love came in many colours.

'I have got you a new pair of beautiful slippers. You will be wearing them to school,' she said.

I nodded happily. Eagerly, I stretched to see the slippers. She turned to a *Ghana-must-go* bag that was kept at the foot of our bed and brought out a pair of blue-spotted red bathroom slippers.

'You like them?'

'Yes Mama,' I said. I quickly slipped my feet into them excitedly.

'No. Wait. You are putting them on the wrong feet.'

While I changed the slippers, Mama quickly went to her cloth-hanger. She began to dress up.

Her cloth-hanger was merely a rope that was tied on two points of the mud wall. Despite, Mama always arranged her clothes on it neatly. Except for her two wrappers which were in the *Ghana-must-go,* all her blouses hung neatly on the rope. She picked a white headscarf with an image of Mother Mary on it from the hanger and tied her cornrows. Soo, she was done dressing up. She went to a pot which was kept beside the water pot and brought me some of the leftover yam from the previous night. She had warmed the yam this morning. She prayed over the food and we began to eat.

We left the hut immediately after eating. Mama led the way out of the hut, holding my hand behind her. When we approached Eliza's hut, Mama turned and cautioned, 'You will not be a rude child at school, will you?' I shook my head quietly.

We arrived Eliza's hut and Mama greeted. However, there was no response. She called out again but silence returned for her greetings. It appeared there was no one in the hut. Eliza had made fire not too far from the hut. I could see a pot of soup warming up on fire. There was also a smoked clay-pot beside the door. One of Eliza's brown-bodied-white-neck nanny goats was picking some yam peels near the clay-pot.

We were now walking towards the cashew tree. Father Gregory always parked his CG125 motorcycle under the tree. The motorcycle was not there now. It was when we had just passed the spot that we saw Eliza come out of the toilet, a little round hut.

'Are you going to school already?' She asked Mama from the distance.

'Yes-o. We are,' Mama replied. 'How is your husband? I thought he was inside the hut but when I greeted, I got no response,' she added.

'He is fine,' Eliza answered. 'He left the house early this morning to Mbaikyo to find out if his pension has been paid.'

Eliza approached us. She had on a short wrapper that only covered her from breast to knee. I could see the scapular she wore had made a distinctive mark on her skin around her neck.

Eliza laughed. She just laughed to herself – like she did days ago when husband called her a bush woman. Eliza had refused to go to the farm that day. She had complained that grass caused her skin to itch, and laughed. 'How did I end up with this ignoramus girl?' Her husband asked Mama.

He began to tell Mama how his wife Eliza was like Obasanjo, the chairman of the state pensions board. 'Obasanjo is only happy when praise-singers sing him praises, and Eliza too loves luxuriant praises.' But Mama did not let me listen much; she instructed me to go into our hut until she called me out later.

Eliza came. She held my hand. 'Sometimes I wonder how he is growing so fast like he is being watered.'

'I wonder too,' Mama returned. 'Maybe he is growing so fast because I feed him with too much water yam!' They both laughed lightly. 'We are already late for school. We should be going already,' Mama said. She thanked Eliza and we began to walk away.

I held on to Mama's index finger firmly as we went. Soon, we had walked past the cashew tree. We were almost taking a right turn at the end of the church hall. There, I saw a dog urinating near a shrub. It was steering as we approached.

'Ma-ma,' I called.

'Yes—,' she answered.

'Do dogs wash their hands after defecating?'

'No—,' she said almost silently.

'Mama, why don't they wash their hands? Don't they have hands?'

'No,' she said.

I feared that the dog could suddenly attack us. Mama looked unbothered. At the same time, I wanted to ask Mama why dogs could see evil spirits at night. I felt I would get no attention. As we approached the dog, it began to ran away. Soon, we had passed the shrub where it had urinated. The path from the shrub became bushy. The grasses around were still wet with dew. I could hear the sound of water gurgling through a gully. There was a gully nearby. Presently, we were skirting around the school football field.

From the football field, I could see some children sitting in a classroom. When we got to the classroom, I noticed a part of its old clay walls had collapsed at the back. The roof of the classroom was made of thatch and it tilted precariously towards the collapsed wall. Beside was another room just like it. The only reason the thatched roof didn't come right off the building was because it was supported by three bamboo poles. This was where my education would kick off in life. When we approached the door, my heart started thumping so much. I could not quickly notice that the door had no door frame. Unlike our hut; it was just an oblong opening. The two big windows were without frames as well.

Mama bent and peeped inside the room. She spoke with a man who sat inside the classroom, seeking permission. We entered. From the back of the class I could hear the sobbing of a child.

'Good morning sir,' Mama greeted the man. My eyes went wandering around the premises from where I stood behind her sucking my little finger in fear. I had seen the whip on the man's table. My heart jolted with more fear.

Mama pulled me forward. 'This is my son,' she said. 'Father Gregory has asked me to bring him to you for enrolment.'

The man stared at me for a while before he cleared his throat.

'Cute little man', he said, before asking. 'What is your name?' He asked.

I stuttered and tears began to gather in my eyes.

He seemed to become surprised but asked again, 'What is your name?'

I wished I could say something. Regrettably, the words dissolved before my lips could even open. Instead, I turned to Mama at the verge of sobbing. Mama snarled 'Aondoakaa, don't you know your name?'

'My name is… my name is A-ondo-a-kaa,' I sobbed. At that moment, a little girl's cry came from the back of the room as well. I turned and looked. It the brief moment our eyes met, her image stock in my mind. I would later realize that the girl was Tabitha, and she and I in fact had the same father; a man Mama would call Byem.

When I returned to look at the man across the table, he lifted his cane and banged the tabletop. He apologized to Mama. 'These children can sometimes cry like that.' His eyes, moving from Mama, settled on me again. 'What is your father's name, Aondoakaa?' His voice was rather hoarse, and almost raised.

But I was mute again.

'He will catch up quickly. My boy is very intelligent, Teacher,' she pleaded.

Teacher was obviously disappointed. To save herself, Mama screamed, 'Tell Sir Teacher your name, foolish boy!' She gave a brief cautioning look because adding, 'And stop embarrassing me.'

'My father's name is F-a-d-a,' I stuttered.

Sir Teacher stared at Mama, certainly wondering what I was saying. But Mama's cheeks rather sagged. "Fada" was how Father Gregory was called by people who could not pronounce "Father" very well. Over time, it became the white priest's signature name. As a matter of fact, Father Gregory had already stayed in Akan for over ten harmattan seasons. No one called him Father Gregory any longer. 'You must also always call him Fada,' Mama always insisted.

As a boy growing up under the white priest, I thought he was my biological father. But now, pulled my ear, 'Why are you embarrassing me, foolish boy?'

Mama turned to Sir Teacher, and feigning a smile she said: 'His father's name is Adi Byem.'

Teacher smiled before he continued with further questions. Thankfully Mama took up the rest of the interview and supplied the answers. When the man was done with questioning, he picked a book and wrote a few things in it. That was the end of the enrolment process.

'He can start school immediately if he is ready, Madam,' Teacher said.

'Sure he is, Sir,' Mama answered.

I am sure Mama noticed that I did not want to start school anymore. I did not like this man that had so many names; "Sir" "Teacher" and "Sir Teacher". Worse, I disliked the cane on his table. But I could not say so to Mama because she would break my head. Mama thanked the man. She quickly dragged me outside the classroom. 'Do not to fight or play in the class,' she reminded. Turning to go, she added, 'And, listen, your father's name is not Fada. Do you hear me? Your father's name is Byem! That is what you must tell everyone when asked.' She rubbed my head, 'Go back into your class.' With that, she turned and began to walk briskly away.

Mama never walked slowly, except when I was walking with her. She always walked as if she was chasing after something. Eliza's husband had once said she would make a good soldier; but Mama only laughed over it.

I stood there staring as Mama walked away. My eyes began to be filled with tears again. Some distance away, she turned and caught me still standing there like a dry bamboo pole, motionless. 'Go into your class!' came her voice.

I turned and began to walk back into the classroom with heavy steps. My left thumb was in my mouth. The right hand was pulling the bottom button of my shirt.

From that day, my academic journey started at St. Winifred Catholic Primary School in Akan. Akan was very much still a village miles away from the foot of concrete modernization.

There too, my fate began. My life would mostly become full of regrets.

I took a step, entered into the class and stood by the door.

I took a seat at the back of the classroom. The seats in this classroom were hewn rocks arranged in rolls and columns. My feet seemed to be sinking in the sandy floor like I was standing on quicksand. Sir Teacher went to a blackboard and began to write on it with white chalk. When he had written a letter, he turned half facing us, pointed to the writing on the blackboard with the cane held in his hand. He said, 'All of you repeat after me, Ay.'

'Eeeh,' we chorused.

'Ay,' he said again.

'Eeeh,' we chorused.

'Ay.'

'Eeeh,' we chorused.

He kept reading out the writing on the blackboard, asking us to repeat after him. Each time, we did.

After sometime, he wrote another symbol and half facing us again, he asked us to say after him, 'Bee.'

'Biii,' we chorused, stretching the i's into polyphonic tunes.

But a boy who sat beside me, whom I would later know by name as Aker, would not repeat. Rather, he was drawing a human figure on the floor with his finger.

'Bee,' the teacher said again.

The boy was still drawing. His drawing was coming on fine and I couldn't help but stare at it. I was staring hard at him and at some point, he stopped the drawing and stared back at me for a while. He hissed. Abruptly, he fetched a handful of sand on the floor and threw it at me.

'Aondoakaa Fada! What are you staring at?  You fool!' He said fuming. Particles of the dust got into my eyes. At once I shut my eyes gave a scream, rubbing out the sand grains. When I opened my eyes eventually, he stuck his tongue out at me. Looking up at Teacher, I began to cry.

'What monkey is crying there? Shut up!' The teacher's voice

came as he started walking towards me with a cane in his hand. The troublesome boy rolled his tongue at me again. I cried even louder. Tears were still running down my cheeks when Teacher got to me. He was so angry that he raised his whip high in the air and brought it down on my back heavily. When his whip connected with my back again, I sprinted away from my seat and howled at the top of my voice, arching my back in pain.

'Monkey, shut up!' he shouted angrily but I couldn't help crying.

Aker was still rolling his tongue at me when Teacher caught him. He brought down the weight of the cane on the boy's head.

'Aker,' the man called, fuming. 'You stubborn boy, what did you just do?' The rascal twisted in pain without crying and simply swore that he did nothing wrong to me. Teacher drew back a bit from Aker and to my surprise, he stared at the boy silently for a while, turned and walked back to the blackboard. When he was in front of the class, I held the ear of my shirt and dried my tears, making a mental note to tell Mama that Aker called me Aondoakaa Fada and threw dust in my face. I was sure Mama would come to school and beat him up.

Now, Teacher had written something again, 'See!' he said.

'Ciii!' we repeated.

But Aker was not going to say a word. He sat solidly beside me, like a log of wood.

The bell rang, indicating that school had closed for the day. Happy voices of children rent the air. Teacher led us and we recited the Lord's Prayer at the top of our voices. After the Lord's Prayer, my classmates began to run out of the classroom. They were shouting in glee. I was the last to leave the room. When outside, I saw Aker running towards the football field. On the other side of the field was a citrus orchard. Beside were some pawpaw and coconut trees that thinned into the horizon.

Instead of going across the field, Aker stopped where a group of children were walking home along the edge of the field. Soon I found out the reason he had run. The group was following an elderly man who was pushing a bicycle along the path. A goatskin bag hung from the old man's shoulder. The children trailed the old man, chanting 'Mata Geri! Mata Geri!' And each time they chanted, the old man answered, 'Ooou!' in a voice cracked with age.

'Mata Geri, how does a cow cry?' a child asked.

'A cow cries *mooooou...*' The old man replied. The children laughed happily.

'Mata Geri,' another child called.

'Oooooou!' He answered again.

'Mata Geri, how does a goat cry?' The child inquired.

'A goat cries *miaan – miaan*!' The children burst into laughter again.

'Mata Geri!' another child called.

'Ooooooou!' The old one answered, his trembling hands firmly gripped the handle of the bicycle and the goatskin bag hung perfectly on his shoulder.

'Mata Geri, how does a sheep cry?' The child inquired.

'A sheep cries *meeeeeh*!' He said. And yet again, the children burst into laughter. I had almost caught up with the group now. Aker called, 'Mata Geri!' His voice rang out distinctively.

'Oooou!' The old man answered again.

'Mata Geri, how does a tortoise cry?'

'A tortoise… A tortoise is hungry, so she holds her little one and runs away!' The children laughed endlessly.

We got to the shrub where Mama and I had seen a dog urinate that morning. I turned and headed home following a sandy path by the church-hall. The sun burnt my skin. Beads of sweat coated my face. The children continued to follow the old man as he pushed his bicycle and supply responses to their questions.

When I got home, I saw Eliza's husband's bicycle leaning against a cashew tree beside their hut. However, there was nobody in the compound. I saw one of Eliza's goats grazing behind my mother's hut. There was also a rooster chasing a hen.

Eliza came out of her hut. She scampered towards me when she saw me. 'Aondoakaa! Aondoakaa! Aondoakaa!' She called as she ran towards me. She raised me into the air.

'School man! Are you hungry?' She asked.

I nodded.

'Did you eat before you left for school?'

I nodded.

She returned me to the ground, dished a smile. 'I have cooked food. Let's go and eat. Your mother has gone to buy ingredients for soup in the market. She will be back soon. You hear?' I nodded. Eliza held me by the hand. She led me into her hut where I sat on a small wooden stool. She served me boiled yam and palm oil stew.

'Did you learn anything in school?' she asked.

I nodded.

'What did you learn?'

'Eeeeh, biii, hef, ciii, hef.'

She smiled generously. 'Did you learn all that today?'

I nodded.

Eliza's husband's voice came from outside the hut. He greeted my mother.

'Mama is back,' I said.

'Finish your food,' Eliza replied.

Her husband was bare-chested. There was a shirt hanging from his left shoulder. He pushed the door which was left ajar and came in. He was oozing of alcohol. I stood and greeted him, bowing respectfully as Mama had instructed that I always do when I greeted an elder. The man gave no response. Instead, he walked to the bed and sat on its edge. His chest heaved as he took deep breaths. Then he began to rant: His pension for the month was not paid again!

'Obasanjo is a coward!' The man said throatily. 'I say Obasanjo is a coward!' This time it was with a gruffer voice.

Eliza stood near the door. She stared at her husband quietly. This was not the first time he would return from the Pensions Board and start heaping insults on the board chairman, Mr. Obasanjo. He always did, and Eliza had become used to it. She would tell my mother that it was military madness. 'Every ex-soldier who had fought the Nigeria-Biafra War has it in him,' she would add.

'Where was the ignoramus Obasanjo during the Biafra War? Where was he when we were shooting heavy machine guns gam-gam-gam? Where was the ignoramus coward? Did we not see real death during the war? But as for the ignoramus, he vamoosed to Liberia to fight a "chicken war" in the name of United Nation's peace-mission. We combated in the real war here! And I was in the warfront fighting for this geographical entity called Nigeria. But as for the rapscallion ignoramus, he vamoosed.

'Captain Dingwa would bear witness to what our eyes saw, were he alive today. He would tell how for two and half days, February in 1968—that was the month—how we were surrounded, cordoned as a matter of fact, by a very angry-heart Biafran troop. Death hung over our trenches and opened its eyes at us. Death hung and waited.

'The Biafran troop comprised several *small pikin sojas* who hardly past twelve years old, and only God knows that those ones dangerous well well in a troop. They could blast a man's head *fiap!* They shot even when only nah housefly buzzed! They would just blast gun.'

He demonstrated, as if he held a gun pointing at me.

'So, we were in trenches—Captain Dingwa and one Hausa Private, and me. Death opened its eyes at us. But as good *sojas*, who swear oath to maintain this country, no matter the tough situation, we gallantly faced that time to defeat the enemy or better the enemy kill us. Our chance to defeat the enemy was small, very slim. We had no water remaining with us, no food and worst of all, we had no bullets, except for the Private who had only two or three left in his gun. But an intelligent *soja* does not only survive by the gun, he also uses his head! A foolish *soja*, like Obasanjo, would at such a time open fire at the enemy, and subdue a few men then fall. But we avoided using such a plan. Did we fear death? No! Say who die?

'Captain Dingwa was the one in the trench next to mine. We waited. Day one, we waited. Day two, the Captain no longer fit hold his thirst. He pulled out of the pit to go get water from nearby banana plant stem. That was where he was demolished. A devilish grenade flew *fiaaaa* past over my trench, and in the blink of my eye, as I raised my head a little and peeped, I saw that Captain Dingwa was demolished. It pained me to lose such a *soja-soja* as Captain. But I only lowered myself back inside the pit and weep! Yes, I wept for my life. I wept like a foolish woman who her husband batters! Such moments come, even for a *soja*. Where was Obansajo then? Where was the rapscallion ignoramus?'

Eliza was quiet, so was I.

'Now, he is made the chairman of the Pensions Board by ordinary civilians, and he thinks he can embezzle our pension! Say who die? He cannot! This Obasanjo, this canaille, this rabble property of syndicating perpetual disparity, he cannot! The coward can't. I will personally shoot him in the *nyash*! Hmmuh!'

The man turned to Eliza, his chest rising and falling rapidly, 'You foolish woman! Must I beg you to bring my food?' He yelled. I shuddered with fear. The plate of yam I was holding fell from my hand to the floor.

I knew another fight between the man and Eliza was not far. Eliza knew this too. Her eyes roved here and there in fear. 'Did you buy soup when you were leaving this house to go and drink your life out with your mad friends?' Eliza asked and ran out of the room like a rat at the sight of a cat.

I sat there on the stool trembling. The fuming man hissed. He stood up and drew a machete that hung on the roof in a goatskin sheath. Then, he ran out. My heart was thumping in fear. Soon, I heard Eliza screaming and running around the compound. But not long enough, she was quiet.

To my relief, Mama came into the hut. She fetched me out. I saw Eliza standing behind Father Gregory with only a wrapper tied round her bosom. Her husband stood in front of the priest. He was panting impatiently. The machete was still in his hand.

Mama went to meet them as the priest spoke to Eliza's husband.

'Father Gregory,' the man called, 'let me tell you something. One should not count the teeth of a goat with one's finger just because the goat does not bite like a rattle snake. But if arrogance fills the head and one counts the teeth of a goat with one's fingers, well then, the occasion waits when arrogance would drive the finger to the rattle snake's mouth! This foolish animal takes my gentility these days for foolishness! I will show her that I am still a *soja*!' The man's eyes were blood-shot as he continued to fume with rage.

He drew closer with the machete. Father Gregory, a well-built man in his late forties, knocked off the machete from his hand. Of course, no matter how angry the ex-soldier was, he knew his limits when Father Gregory was around. Later that day, when things became calm, Fada summoned the man and cautioned him. Beating up a woman was sinful in God's eye, the priest emphasized.

Mama pulled Eliza aside and took her by the hand into.

In our hut, she took off my clothes, wore me a pair of shorts. She asked me to climb into the bed and sleep.

Eliza sat unsteadily on the edge of the bed.

Soon, Mama left the hut to cook some food.

Eliza drew closer. She smiled, gave a grinned and thrust her left hand into my shorts and touched my *ajuju*. She began to caress it.

'Very big. Like a big tuber of yam…'

Mama pushed the door and came in. I had just woken from my nap. Eliza was no longer in the room. I sat up, yawned, and greeted Mama. She returned my greeting casually and continued towards the water pot. Just by the water pot, a cockroach was feeding on a drop of palm-oil on the floor. Its antenna wagged in the air. The insect appeared to sense Mama's presence. It quickly slipped under the water-pot. I could still see its antenna.

Mama hurried out of the hut. She returned with a broom in hand. With it, she swept the cockroach out of hiding. As the cockroach scurried across the room in search of another hiding place, I jumped out of bed and squashed it with one of my slippers. The bug spread its wings, quivered momentarily and lay still. 'Pick it by its wings and throw it outside', Mama said. I picked it up and threw it out through the door, then returned into the room. 'Go and wash your hands', Mama said.

When I was washing my hands in a bowl outside the hut, I remembered how Aker had called me Aondoakaa Fada in school. I got back into the hut and told Mama about the incident.

'Mama, a boy in my class called me Aondoakaa Fada while Teacher was *talking*. The boy's name is Aker. He also threw dust at me,' I reported.

'What happened?' Her face was grim as she enquired.

'Aker was making a sketch with his finger on the ground. When I looked at it, he called me Aondoakaa Fada'.

'Don't mind Aker, he is a foolish boy,' Mama said, the grimness fading off her face. She turned to the basket on the floor, fetched a plate from it and was walking out of the hut when she stopped at the door, turned towards me and said, 'Your father's name is Adi Byem, not Fada.' With this said, she walked out of the hut. Later that evening, Mama would explain that Father Gregory was not my father. He was only a kind priest who offered us accommodation while she assisted him with domestic duties. The word Fada, an altered form of father, was only a title for a Catholic priest.

When Mama came into the room again, she brought *luam*. She prepared the yam paste by pounding well cooked peeled yams in a mortar. This was eaten by molding a small ball at a time, dipping into soup and swallowing. I went to the water pot and brought drinking water in a cup.

'Pray before you eat,' she instructed me before walking out of the room. I prayed and began to eat the food. When I had completely finished the mound, I took the plates out of the hut. At the door, I saw the lifeless insect that I had crushed earlier. A colony of ants had begun to dismember the body and haul the parts away.

## II

Father Gregory sat in front of his house on a wooden chair close to the porch of the building. He was reading his Bible. Although we lived in the same compound separated only by a wide empty land, Fada's building was not like ours which were round huts with mud walls and spear-grass roofs. His was a beautiful rectangular building with a zinc roof. The priest looked up from the Bible and saw me. He beckoned. I went to him. 'Have you started school?' He asked. I nodded that I had. The man always had an air of excitement; he wore a spirited smile. This was one of the things that endear him to many.

'Good evening Father', I greeted; bowing respectfully.

'My boy!' He stretched his hand and reached for my left hand. 'Did you learn anything in school today?' He asked.

I nodded.

'And, what did you learn?' He continued.

'Eaaay, Biiiii, Siiiii, Hef, Diii, Heff.'

'Impressive!' He edged forward on his seat, dropping the Bible on a small table beside his chair.

'Did you learn all these today?'

I nodded.

'You have learnt so much already. You're a smart boy!' A light laughter escaped from his face.

At that moment, Eliza came out from her kitchen. She walked across to the back of our hut to unfasten the goat she had tethered there to graze. The sun had set already.

Mama brought out our wooden bench and kept it in front of our hut. She would sit there with Eliza hulling melon seeds late into the night. I would sit with them too, and stare at the moon when I would see Mother Mary and Child Jesus in the moon. I would point to the moon and ask Mama if she saw Mother Mary and Jesus too. But Mama would say, 'You foolish boy, get up and go and sleep. Get up at once.'

But on a rare day, Mama would allow me to sit with them longer when she would say the moon was bright because of the shinning glory of the Holy Mother. This would sometimes make me to wish the moon had fallen from heaven into our compound so I could cut a piece of it and keep in our hut. This way, the glory of the Holy Mother would continue to light our hut.

Eliza dragged her goat to her kitchen. She locked it up. Her husband who was the church catechist had rung the bell for Angelus only an hour earlier. He was now gone to meet his retired soldier friends at the palm-wine place.

'Go put on a shirt, the evening is getting cold,' Father Gregory said, tapping my shoulder. I turned and began to walk away happily.

Mama had gone to gather *Bokpari* bush. She would burn it in our hut to drive mosquitoes away. Soon, she returned with the plants and gave me some. 'Keep them under the bench,' she pointed to the bench that she kept in front of our hut. I took the *Bokpari,* kept them under the bench and sat on it, staring up into the sky, watching the moon as it emerged. Soon, Eliza joined me.

Mama had fetched water from a ground well that was dug beside Fada's cottage. She invited me to take my bath. 'Go and sleep so you will wake up early enough to be in school on time tomorrow', she said after I had bathed.

From the next day, waking up early, doing my share of domestic chores, and going to school became a routine.

In school, Aker and I soon became close friends; we played together during the daily long and short breaks.

One evening, Mama and I went to the market where we saw Tabi, the girl in my class, sitting beside a woman. We went to meet the woman whom Mama chatted with for long before we left. 'Mama, Tabi and I are classmates', I said as we walked away. 'Tabi is in fact your sister. She is staying with your father, Byem, in the village,' Mama replied. I did not quite understand what Mama meant. And neither bothered. But in school, my relationship with Tabi gradually became richer. Once often, I would invite her to join Aker and me to play during the breaks.

Aker continued sitting next to me in class and we continued to play at every opportunity. The exciting life continued until we left St. Winifred Catholic Primary School.

After I had completed primary school and was waiting for my First School Leaving Certificate (FSLC), I stayed at home and helped Mama with farm work and domestic chores. I was now twelve years old. One evening, I was making ridges at the back of our hut for Mama. She would plant guinea corn seeds on them. Eliza's husband returned from the Pensions Board on his Raleigh bicycle. The man was whistling as he pushed the bicycle pedals sluggishly into the compound. He rang the bicycle bell again and again. I stood up and greeted him in the distance as he made his way to the cashew tree. He waved his left hand at me continually. His right hand gripped the bicycle handlebar firmly. Even though it was not yet dark, he purposefully switched on the headlight of the bicycle. Each time the man returned from the Pensions Board that excited, one needed not to be told that his pension was paid. He climbed off his bicycle and leaned it against the cashew tree.

He untied a parcel that was wrapped in fresh *luaegh* leaves from the bicycle pannier rack. It was probably meat which he had bought at the market on his way home. He removed his hat and held it in his right hand. He balanced the parcel carefully in the left, walked majestically to their hut.

Eliza came out from the hut, saluted her man excitedly, and collected both the hat and the parcel. Eliza looked pregnant; her belly was protruded. They had waited seven years for this pregnancy.

The evening suddenly became cloudy. Soon, it began to rain lightly. I ran and took shelter in our hut. There was sporadic lightening. Soon, it was accompanied by intermittent rumbling of thunder. I saw Eliza run into the rain to her kitchen where she began making a fire.

When twilight began to give way to the dark night, I went to the bathroom and took my bath. In a while, I returned into the hut. *'Mama is probably trapped by the rain as she is not back from the market,'* I thought as I lit the lantern. I went to the rope where we hung our clothes and picked a pair of shorts and a *danshiki* to wear. At the moment, I noticed movements at the door of the hut. As I hurriedly wore the shorts, a knock followed. The door creaked open. Eliza walked in. She smiled coquettishly when she saw that I was dressing up hurriedly.

'What are you hiding from me?' she asked, laughing lightly.

I was mute.

'You better know you are turning into a man!' she said, snorting. I caught my breath. I always did each time she said such things.

'Your mother said to me this morning that you will be going to Mbaikyo for secondary school...' she continued. I didn't say anything. Just then, the sound of Father Gregory's motorcycle reached us from the distance as he rode home. I knew Eliza was in the hut for something else. But upon hearing the sound of the motorcycle, she turned and picked a plastic dish where Mama kept salt and hurriedly left the room. I let out a sigh of relief. The motorcycle rode into the compound and stopped. I went to the door and peeped. Father Gregory was carrying Mama at the back of the motorcycle. She climbed down.

Eliza came out from her kitchen. She welcomed Father Gregory and Mama. The priest walked into his room while Mama came in the drizzle into our hut. Her clothes were all wet. I saluted her, bowing.

'My son...' she greeted as she sat on the bench.

As if the words were waiting in her mind impatiently, she took a deep breath and said, 'At last, you will be going to Mbaikyo tomorrow morning for your secondary school!' It was something I knew already, but it still sounded a bit shocking. I just stared and said nothing.

I had grown to be so close to my mother that the thought of leaving her for Mbaikyo scared me. While I was lost in thought, Mama coughed twice and said, 'You should be happy.'

'Mama, you are cold...' I said calmly.

'I am alright...' she coughed again, 'My throat itches.'

'Can I warm some water for you to bath?'

She shook her head, 'I am alright.'

I returned to the bench and joined her. 'Mama, I am happy that I will be furthering my education but I wonder who will be helping you on the farm in my absence.'

'Little frog, do not worry yourself to climb the tree for food,' she said and smiled. The feigned smile died out and she continued, 'A frog's food will never climb a tree. But even if it does, it must fall back to the earth.'

Mama never used proverbs much, except when her heart was heavy. I grew up to realize that proverbs were not like a mirror which every woman could use indiscriminately; it was not very proper for a woman to use proverbs because proverbs were the chewing stick with which men cleaned their minds. It was thus odd for a woman to be heard speaking in proverbs.

'Mama, you have said this proverb a number of times to me...'

'Yes, I want you to know that life doesn't always give one what one wants. I have always wanted you to be very educated. I have always wanted you to acquire the education which I did not get. I always thank the Virgin Mother for her mercies, for bringing us to Fada who is very much willing to support your education,' she sighed.

As Mama continued speaking to me that evening, she said if I was well educated, I would make a difference in our lives; I would light my lamp and find my way in life. She also told me how she had come to stay with the priest when her uncle, Tabi's father, had raped her and her relatives threw her out, calling her names as the man denied the rape and the resultant pregnancy.

Mama told me how her widowed mother could not endure the shame. She died soon after. What she could not tell me was that we were considered outcasts in our village; because virginity was considered so sacred that for a young unmarried woman to suddenly become pregnant was completely unwelcome. As I would learn in years to come, if a girl was 'so undisciplined' as to lose her virginity, she had to face the music all her life. The question no one ever asked or answered was what happened to the man who played the drums.

Mama was thus homeless. She was miserable when the God-sent Father Gregory found her. Father Gregory brought her to stay in the church house. Initially, the church community did not welcome her stay. But Father Gregory insisted that God had forgiven Mama so no one had the right to condemn her.

When I was born, Mama said, she had almost made up her mind that I would answer Father Gregory's name. It was the only way she could show her appreciation for the man's kindness. Mama said she knew I was a blessing, not a curse. So she named me 'Aondoakaa', meaning God will speak. And she had vowed, right at my birth, that I would have education at all cost. As she spoke, a tear fell from her left eye and rolled down her cheek. She quickly turned her face away, held the edge of her wrapper and wiped the cheek. She did not want me to see her misery. As I listened my heart grew heavy, and so did my eyes.

It had drizzled and the night was cold. Mama did not sit with Eliza outside this evening. Instead, when she realized how the story she was telling was throwing me off, she went on to ask me how much work I had done on the farm in the evening.

'I have almost finished making all the heaps', I said.

'Oh, my son, thank you! I will complete the work tomorrow', Mama replied.

She left the hut to have her bath. I lay on a mat on the floor and lay staring up at the roof until sleep enveloped me.

The following morning, a cockcrow woke me up. Mama was up and about, outside the hut. I got up from the mat and noticed that all my personal effects had been arranged in a new *Ghana-must-go* and kept on the bench. On getting outside the hut, I saw Eliza coming out from her kitchen with Mama behind her. I went to them and saluted them. They responded to my greetings cheerfully.

'He will be going to Mbaikyo today,' Eliza said and chuckled.

Mama smiled, 'Yes, he is' she said calmly. Her face soon lost expression. I turned away from the duo and went in search of a broom to sweep the compound.

As I began to sweep the compound, Mama called and said that I should not sweep at night; that I would invite evil spirits. 'It isn't daylight yet,' she cautioned. I returned the broom and left for the hut to wait until it was bright.

When it was no longer dark, I came out of the room and swept the compound before going to take my bath. Father Gregory would take me to Mbaikyo soon. By the time I was through with breakfast, Fada was already waiting, his motorcycle steaming with grey smoke in front of his house.

Eliza came out from her kitchen with her wrapper tied round her chest. She was rubbing her left eye with the back of her hand. She came and stood, arms akimbo, beside the motorcycle. Father Gregory came out and met me by the motorcycle. I greeted him and bowed. He answered my greetings, climbing the motorcycle. He sat on the front V-Shape seat while I climbed and sat behind him. Mama came running from our hut. She was supporting her breasts with one hand and holding a plastic bag in the other. 'Will you leave your shoes behind?' she asked. Eliza laughed. It was not clear to me whether the sound Eliza made came from her mouth or nose because it was a dry laugh. I turned to Mama and smiled, receiving the plastic bag from her.

Father Gregory started the engine of the motorcycle and it began to rumble. I placed the plastic bag firmly on my lap. My excitement at climbing a motorcycle for the first time in my life and going to Mbaikyo was married with fear. Eliza turned to my mother and laughed. In her laughter, I saw how much she was missing me already. Mama stood, staring helplessly. I am sure there was much on her mind.

Father Gregory throttled the motorcycle and we began to move slowly toward the church hall. The atmosphere was pleasantly calm. I turned and waved at Mama. Eliza and Mama waved back. Soon, we were off the church premises. We rode past the primary school and were soon riding through a sandy country road. It was quiet long before we came across a group of men who were on their way to their farm; each carried a big hoe on his shoulder. Two or three also carried machetes. The men withdrew to the shoulder of the bushy road as they greeted, 'Fada! Fada! Fada!' Father Gregory answered them by blowing the motorcycle horn.

The ear of my shirt flapped under the morning wind as we went.

Long after, we met two elderly women who were returning from the stream with clay pots carefully balanced on their heads. On sighting the motorcycle approaching, they quickly stepped off the road to give us way. When we got to them, they saluted, calling out in cheerful voices, 'Fada!' I wondered how Father Gregory was so well known far away from our compound. He blew the horn again, waving vigorously.

We were riding upland towards a hill. In the distance, I could see a herd of cattle grazing at the foot of the hill. A boy of about my age stood nearby, watching over a herd. As we drew closer, I could tell that he was Fulani from his wicker hat, a jar of water, and club that hung across his shoulders.

The country road had become narrower and less sandy. The vegetation too had thinned to a few scanty grasses and some stunted and tetra-headed trees.

I could hear faint drumbeats filtering through the air from the distance ahead of us. The drum sounds became clearer and I could even hear the voices of women singing to the drumbeats. Father Gregory took a sharp turn to the left and we were suddenly in a small village that had only few huts. Naked children were playing in the sun not quite far from the road. Goats were also grazing. They reminded me of Eliza's goats back home. But soon, I began to think about the woman herself. As we approached a little village market, thoughts of Eliza faded and were replaced by thoughts of Mama.

This village market was not different from the one back home in Akan; there were few trees and *ate* huts just as in Akan market. A woman of about Mama's age sat under one of the trees selling beer, with four young people and an elderly man making a crescent to her. They stared at us as we approached.

Soon, we passed the market and met an old woman on her way to the market. The drumbeats were more distinct now, much nearer so that Father Gregory slowed down the motorcycle and halted. The old woman, on seeing the white man, became very excited. The very fact that his skin was white like an albino made him a strange sight. 'Mama, *msugh u'*, Father Gregory greeted the woman in Tiv. After staying in Akan for over seventeen years, Fada could speak Tiv near perfectly, except that he seemed to pronounce words through his nose. This made the words unusually longer. It was as if he added several R's to each word. When Father Gregory greeted the old woman in Tiv, she became even more excited and replied happily, laughing and calling us her children. Father Gregory then asked why the drums were being played.

'*Gum-or shi ngohol kwase, se lu ember ye,*' the woman responded. Father Gregory laughed lightly after hearing that the celebration was for a young man who had taken another wife. Going by the teachings of the church, for a man to have more than one wife was carnality and a sin; there was nothing to celebrate about it. Fr. Gregory thanked the woman for her explanation, and we continued our journey.

Thoughts of Mama came to my mind again but soon disappeared.

We were on a narrow, dusty road again. The earth became brownish. We were now riding across wood-logs structured into a bridge across a stream. Father Gregory seemed to take more care as he rode across the wooden bridge.

We had just crossed the bridge when I saw an old and broken wooden signboard by the roadside that read, "MBAIKYO HEALTHCARE CENTER." An arrow below the writing pointed to an old building with a rusted zinc roof.

Father Gregory kept on riding. The road was straight now. There were more houses and more people. We got to a town market with tarred roads! A car drove past us and stopped not quite far away. I was staring in wonder.

'Ondokarrrr, this is Mbaikyorrrr,' Father Gregory informed me. 'Your new school is only a short distance from here.' I searched my head for an appropriate response but found none. Eventually, I simply said, 'Yes Fada.'

**Watering Guinea-corn**

### *University of IBRU, Urokpa-West* 

I had completed my secondary school education at Mt. St. Michaels' Catholic College in Mbaikyo one-month shy of clocking eighteen years. That same year, I sat for the University Matriculation Examination (UME) and passed all subjects very well. I was then offered admission to study Religion and Philosophy at the University of IBRU in Urokpa-West.

While I waited for a new academic session to commence, I returned home to Akan and helped Mama on the farm.

During the time I was away for secondary school at Mbaikyo, Mama had developed a painful lump in one of her breasts. She said she noticed the lump the day the pope was shot dead in the Vatican by unknown gunmen. That was two years back. The pain grew worse every passing day. Sometimes the pain would become a moving object that made her cough without ceasing. Despite her condition, Mama was always working on the farm; she had to feed and take care of us. Mama didn't exactly seek medical attention for her ailment. She only drank the juice from fresh *ugwu* leaves and pawpaw roots soaked in holy-water.

Mama told me that Eliza's husband had prescribed the remedy for her and, though it wasn't exactly a cure, it gave her momentary relief.

I suggested that she needed medical attention for permanent relief. But Mama disliked Western medicine. There was a new healthcare centre next to the primary school in Akan. Although it was not fully equipped, Eliza attested to the effectiveness of the centre.

Akan had developed significantly during my absence, even though it was still far behind Mbaikyo. Unlike Mbaikyo, there were no tarred roads in Akan. However, Akan too had started experiencing the sprouting up of new modern houses here and there.

Like Mama, Eliza informed me, the community had not yet accepted Western medication. The people said the tablets they received at the healthcare centre were too tiny to offer cure to ailments. I was sure this view would soon change.

The visible development of Akan was majorly due to the impact of the church. Father Gregory had started a new church-building project. He had also laid the foundation for a house where my mother, Eliza and her husband would move in. Whenever I was not on the farm, I went to assist at the new buildings.

One evening while I was assisting at the building, Father Gregory returned from Mbaikyo. He came straight to supervise the progress of the building.

'The University of IBRU has opened for registration of fresh students. Registration will close in a week's time', he said calmly. Mama was with me, she also heard this great news. But to me, the news was quite disturbing. Despite my eagerness to go to university and gain more education, which was also Mama's earnest desire for me, we hadn't the money that I needed for the registration. There was in fact no means to raise the money quickly. In the night, when we were about to retire to bed, Mama and I prayed for a miracle. A miracle was all we could hope for.

As if the heavens had been waiting for our call, early the next morning help came. Someone came knocking on our door. I got up from the mat where I had slept, went to the door and opened. It was Eliza's husband. 'I want to see your mother', he requested before acknowledging my greeting. Mama came, met him and they stepped away to talk. When she returned to the room, she said, 'Get ready, you are leaving for Urokpa to get your registration done. God has answered our prayer'.

I smiled, not because I believed her but because I felt she was becoming rather too assertive.

'Mama, but we have no money yet', I reminded her.

She turned and waved a bunch of naira notes at me, 'See', she said. Eliza's husband had given her the money. I clasped my hands together, bowed my head and thanked God. Afterwards, I left our room to thank the man.

I got to their hut and knocked at the door. Eliza came and opened and stood with her left hand on the wooden door frame. 'Good morning Eliza. Is your husband in?' I asked.

'No, he is not. He just left for Mbaikyo a while ago', she replied.

Adu, Eliza's little boy whom she had given birth to in my absence, made his way out beside his mother and went to defecate by the banana plants.

'Come inside', Eliza invited me.

'Thank Eliza', I said and turned away.

'Will you not spend small time with me before you travel?', Eliza asked. I was already walking away.

When I returned to our hut, Mama was putting some of my items together in a *Ghana-must-go* bag. She had packed tubers of yams, few clothes, *gari*, palm-oil, and a bottle of Holy Water. 'The water will keep evil spirits away from you', she said, showing me the bottle. 'Sprinkle it around your bed when you get to school'.

I did not offer verbal appreciation, I only stared gratefully. I soon joined her in arranging my books in the bag before hurrying to the bathroom.

Father Gregory was warming his motorcycle outside. Mama went to greet him. When she returned to the hut, I was already dressed.

'Take the bag to the motorcycle: Fada will take you to Mbaikyo where you will get a car to take you to Urokpa-West.' she said.

'But Mama, Fada was supposed to go to Uka this morning, wasn't he?' I asked.

'He wants to drop you off at Mbaikyo, he said so.'

'I thank God for him.'

'Yes, we thank God for him.'

Mama accompanied me out as I took my bag to wait by the motorcycle. Eliza came to meet us. She brought some smoked fish in leaf wraps. 'Take', she said calmly, handed them to me and then returned to their hut. Soon, Father Gregory came to meet me by the motorcycle, dressed in his white cassock.

'Good morning Father', I greeted as he mounted the motorcycle and started it. I joined him. With a single kick, the motorcycle came alive.

Mama began to wave at us even before we started riding away.

The journey to Mbaikyo was shorter this time. This was probably so because I had become familiar with the route. We got to Mbaikyo about a few minutes to eleven o'clock in the morning. We rode straight to the motor-park. From there, Father Gregory would go to Uka. He dropped me at the motor-park and left immediately. Unfortunately, the last vehicle going to Urokpa-West for the day had left. Another would leave the next morning around seven o'clock. I paid the fare, collected a ticket and went to the Catholic Church at Mbaikyo. Father John, the priest at Mbaikyo, had travelled to Makurdi. His cook, Oluche who had been my friend when I was in Mt. St. Michaels, told me the priest was attending a deanery meeting in Makurdi. I stayed with Oluche and slept in his room.

The next day, I took my bath as early as 5a.m and left for the motor-park. The morning was breezy and the clouds heavy. A train was passing through Mbaikyo to Makurdi when I got to the motor-park. It was whistling intermittently. Those trains were said to come from far away Lagos.

It was nearly dawn. The vehicle for Urokpa-West was parked by the shoulder of the road leading to Makurdi. It was a beige Peugeot saloon. An empty can was kept on the roof. On it was written "MBAIKYO TO UROKPA-WEST." I took my bag to the boot, showed my ticket to a shabby young man who was loading luggage into the car. Two passengers had already taken seats in the car. I came and leaned on the right backdoor of the car, staring toward the road. Two motor-park touts were arguing fiercely across the road. They were insulting each other. I wondered what the matter was. Somehow, the sight uninterested me. So, I looked elsewhere to a man hawking wares; kolanuts and cigarettes on a tray.

'Mallam…' I greeted him.

'Aboki,' the man answered, posting a mild smile.

'Do you have bitter-kola?' I asked.

'Bitter-kola, e dey.' He pointed at it on the tray.

I stepped slightly, asked, 'How much is it?'

'Teree, hamsin,' he said.

'Three for fifty naira, you mean?'

'Yes,' his smile was still warm.

I paid and collected the kolanuts. While waiting for him to hand me my balance, he asked, 'Aboki, I no buy cigar?' His smile this time showed a set of spaced brown teeth.

'I don't smoke,' I said.

'Cigar e good for me, wallahi!' he contested, still smiling.

I received for my balance, turned and walked back to the car.

The clouds that had formed were becoming more rain-promising. I got into the car and took a seat. The vehicle was almost full now, except for two unoccupied seats. But soon, two middle-aged men with tribal marks on their cheeks came hurriedly carrying sacks. They took up the vacant seats. The driver joined us after having a short argument over money with the vehicle loader. He started the engine.

The car made a wracking noise. It jerked as the engine picked up. Soon, it began to move. A lady who sat beside me suggested we pray for journey mercies. I bowed my heads. She began to pray. She was not praying calmly like Mama did back home; she started by clapping hands, singing, and then praying vigorously, as if she were arguing with somebody. When she said, 'Our enemies will never see our blood', there was a louder 'Amen'. Finally, she stopped. I made the sign of the cross.

The car was moving very fast. The trees by the road side seemed to run behind our car, as we sped.

It began raining. We wound the glasses up such that only the driver's window had its glasses mid-way up. The driver started playing highlife music from the car stereo. At first, the songs sounded too slow, almost unlikable. But the singer had a fine voice. I leaned against the back-window glass, listened as the song played.

> *My own is one*
> *way*
> *Only a journey of*

*one way*
*A journey simple*
*and straight*
*One way will I*
*goooo*
*Just this one way*
*Tomorrow I*
*shaaall be here*
*no moooore.'*

Staring as the rain splashed the glass window, it became difficult to see into the distance. However, I could see the big lorries that were on their way to Lagos. Our car kept overtaking one after another. I just kept staring through the glass. As we approached a hill, the rain suddenly stopped. Visibility returned. The skies became clear again. The trees continued running behind us. The passenger in the front seat wound down the glass of the front window.

Thoughts of Mama came to my mind again. The pain in her breast troubled me. Afterwards, I began to think about Tabi, my primary school mate and sister. She had moved to Makurdi after primary school. It was Iorfa, an uncle working with the Nigerian Railways that took her over. She had only been to Akan once since then, that once when she promised to get me a mobile phone when I gain admission into the university. The thought of the phone lingered in my mind now.

We had driven past the hill. The rays of the tropical sun could be seen cutting through the blue and grayish skies.

A man who sat in one of the middle seats turned to another and started a conversation. 'My brother,' he said, 'did you hear, there was a bomb attack in Pakistan yesterday? It was said on TV that thirteen people died'.

'That is terrible,' the other man replied.

'We should be grateful we don't have such suicide bombings here in Nigeria,' the former said.

'Yes, we don't have suicide bombings here, but we have our own problems. And I dare say, ours are more horrible. What do you say about the consistency in failure of leadership? Our leaders have drained this country by embezzling and looting oil-money across the shores to "safer" foreign banks! Children and women keep dying from malaria, from curable and preventable diseases. Thousands! After spending more than the required number of years in schools, graduates come out only to find out there are no jobs. Our leaders are there because it is a way to loot public funds. That's it! It is clear that they have fun watching the masses live a life of penury. I have heard that lately, people go to queue up and clap hands for the big politicians to get their palms oiled, just to survive! That's what I heard.' The man cleared his throat, and then apologized.

He continued, 'As head of a household, one can't even pride oneself that he makes food available to his family as he should, except he agrees to join the people who clap hands for politicians. When a man returns home after a hard day and finds a child coiled up on the floor hungry, his mind tears apart.' The first man laughed dryly. 'Indeed, many people are dying, many can't feed! More so, we lack medical care. Tell me, my brother, is this not more terrible than a bomb attack where only few individuals die?' The former speaker nodded in agreement. They continued to cite instances of horror. Sometimes, they found an issue funny and laughed over it for a while.

The car kept moving at a good speed. We were driving through a thick forest of *luaegh* trees. The road had now tapered into a single lane. The shoulders of the road were eaten away by erosion at this point. Our driver kept up the speed of the car. When we drove past the forest. We came to a little town with old buildings. It was basically a linear settlement. The car slowed down as two young men who were hawking petrol in cans called on the driver to buy. Same as it was in Urukpa, the petrol black market was also formidable in this town. Our driver stopped the car by the side of the road. He turned off the engine. We came out. Some of the passengers went to buy drinking water. Others bought roasted corn hawked by young ladies. A few went into the bush to ease themselves. I stood by the car and stared. My bitter-kola had finished long ago.

The sun was at its zenith; it was noon.

Our driver who had gone into the bush too, returned. He entered the car, started the engine. He was honking, indicating that the passengers should hurry back in. A man who returned to the car sighed. 'We're half way through with the journey so far', he said.

All passengers were back in the car, except for one of the men who had facial marks. The man was soon seen running out from the bush, fixing his belt, sweating, and shouting, '*Ejo-eee, ejo la mi-o!*'

The man with whom he had entered the car at Mbaikyo asked, 'Ah, snake! You saw a snake?'

'Ah, a big snake was chasing me!' The man hurried into the car. He was still panting as he tried to fix the buckle of his belt. There was light laughter in the car before people began to console him.

'*Mo sho le wa mi,*' his friend said to him.

'I didn't enter far into the bush!' He protested.

We took off again.

Our driver was a quiet man. Otherwise, the issues discussed simply didn't interest him.

Now, we were driving across a steel bridge. At the end of the bridge, we saw a broken-down station-wagon car. Its driver had placed wet leaves on the road behind the car. This indicated to oncoming vehicles that his had spoilt. The two passengers in the middle-seat of our car began to talk again.

'This is the famous Niger Bridge,' one said.

'Shortly before the Biafran War, a foreign company wanted to site a hydropower plant here that could have supplied power to this country and two neighbouring ones conveniently. But the government turned down the proposal.'

'Maybe that company did not clap hands.' The other man replied and they all laughed heartily. This time, they did not talk for long before the car became silent, except for the music that the driver was playing. The woman who sat beside me had slept off, snoring with her head rested on my shoulder. Whenever our car bumped into a huge pothole, she mumbled something to herself and continued to sleep.

Now, the sun was almost sinking to twilight. In the distance, we could see the lights of a town.

'At last, we are approaching our destination,' a man said. No one gave response. Soon we were in the town. Our car slowed into a park and stopped. We poured out. Night had come already. I went to the boot and brought out my *Ghana-must-go*. I had no idea of where to go from there. I came to the front of the car and stood against it, confused.

Urokpa-West was a big city, I could see this even in the dark. There were crowds of lights shining from electric bulbs here and there. I stood watching the other passengers leave one after the other. Soon, everyone left. Then silence fall upon the motor-park. There could only be heard the chatter of people who were either trying to buy or eat food from a road side vendor.

The driver who had left earlier to buy food for himself returned to the car. He saw that I was still standing there quietly.

'Who are you waiting for?' He asked.

'I came with you from Mbaikyo but cannot trace my way to the university this night. And, I don't even know where to go from here', I replied.

He stared for a while before suggesting I could sleep in the car. 'You can find your way by tomorrow when its day'.

'Thank you sir', I gladly accepted.

I returned my bag into the car, went in and coiled up on the middle-seat. Soon, I slept off.

I was woken by dogs barking into the dead of the night. Some dogs where fighting over spoils. Not far away from the car, a naked mad woman was wandering about.

I could no longer return to sleep, but sat staring into the night. Hours later, I could hear Islamic prayers blaring from megaphones.

A cock crowed. It was dawn. I could see buildings around the market from the car. The electric lamps on the buildings were still shining brightly. Early morning travelers were beginning to gather in the motor park. The driver came to clean it. We greeted each other. 'Thank you, sir, for your kindness', I said, got my bag and left.

A woman was selling *moimoi* nearby. I went to her and asked for water to wash my mouth, which she gave me. Having washed my mouth, I inquired where I could get a bus to the university. She let her son lead me to a road where I would board a bus to the school.

The first three buses that came around were filled up. Otherwise, they would not carry me because I had luggage. Fortunately, the fourth one was almost empty and was going to the university. I stopped it and hopped in.

As the bus went, I stared. I was so fascinated by the magnificent buildings. A particular building seemed to me to be touching the skies. There were several storey buildings, unlike in Mbaikyo where there was just one in the entire town. Most of the buildings here had electric lights brightly shinning on them. They were unlike the once in Mbaikyo. One could see poles bearing sagging cables stretched into the distance, crisscrossing others. There were many cars and buses, and big roundabouts. I like the city at once.

What intrigued me the most about this magnificent city was that almost all the roads and streets were tarred. Later, I would learn that Urokpa-West was not far from Lagos. In Eliza's husband's words, Lagos was just a stone-throw from Urokpa-West. During the war, he said, a certain captain from their troop would shout in Urokpa-West and one would hear him in Lagos.

I wondered how the drivers knew this vast town so well that they were not missing their way. I liked the bus ride just as I fell in love with the town, even though the bus was old.

After sometime, the town gave way to quietness. The buildings became scanty. There were now long stretches of bush separating buildings. Suddenly, we were at the university gate. A big white signboard by the gate read, "WELCOME TO UNIVERSITY OF IBRU – The Pace Setting University of the Country." I found this inscription delightful. I did not know why, but I truly did. It however also raised some fears in me, a feeling of inadequacy.

As we drove through the gate, two security men saluted the driver. The driver blared his horn several times, pulled an old naira note from his breast pocket, squeezed and threw it at them. 'Baaba! Baaba! Baaba!' the men kept hailing until we passed the gate.

Almost half a kilometer into the school, the bus stopped. We alighted. I went to the boot and got my *Ghana-must-go* bag out. The bus turned and headed back to town. Everyone left the spot where we alighted. I remained there, just confused. I had no slight idea of where to go. I felt like a goat that had been dragged from a village to a market square. My heart began to thump furiously.

Mama's advice came to my mind: 'Talk to someone when you are lost.'

An elderly man of Eliza's husband's age was waking my way. I approached him and greeted, 'Good morning sir'. To my embarrassment, my melancholic front slipped. A tear drop fell from my left eye down the cheek into my shirt. The man appeared confused that I had suddenly began crying.

'What the matter?' He asked.

'I am a new student sir. And, I don't know how to find my way around,' I stuttered.

He smiled. 'What do you want to do then?'

'I want to do my registration, sir.'

'Do you have accommodation yet?'

'No sir.' I answered.

'Well, I see. But how do you go about your registration with this bag on you? I mean, the registration points are far apart. You can't carry the bag all around.'

I gaped at him.

'I am a lecturer here. Come with me, you can keep your bag at my place. I stay nearby.'

I swallowed hard and thanked the man. 'It is nothing at all,' he said.

I lifted my bag to my head and followed him, thinking of Mama as we went.

University of IBRU was a very large school. There were several buildings and a lot of students. The university has two campuses half a kilometer apart; a main and a mini campus. Both campuses were linked by a single-lane road.

That first day in the university, I noticed that the edges of the road that linked the two campuses had been washed away at several places. As one walked along the road leading to the main campus where the administrative block was situated, one would come across an empty flat field and a stream. Beyond this field stood a little hill. A few billboards were erected on the edge of the field. "PLAY SAFE, AIDS IS REAL," one read. "FACE YOUR FUTURE, SAY NO TO CAMPUS CULTISM AND EXAM MALPRACTICE," was the inscription on another billboard. There were also signboards of banks. After the signboards was a Coca-cola Park.

The first building in the main campus was a tall, white architectural piece; the library. Just beside the library was the auditorium. This was where the registration for fresh students was done. I walked into this auditorium.

The registration process in the auditorium lasted for hours. It was from the morning to late afternoon. We had been on queues, from one table to another. When I was through with the registration, I was allocated accommodation. It was a bed-space in Hostel Block C, Room 24. Even though I was exhausted, I hurried to the hostel where I collected a 2.5 x 6 feet mattress from the hostel administrator. That evening, I moved in. The room was downstairs. Very few students had moved in so far.

A week later, there was an orientation lecture for fresh students. It was scheduled for Monday at 9a.m. I took my bath, left the hostel and made for the auditorium by 9:23. By the time I got to the auditorium, the programme had already started. The hall was almost filled to capacity. About two thousand fresh students had been admitted this year. Almost all were in attendance.

Though there were some vacant seats in the hall, some students deliberately stood behind the hall, chatting with friends.

A play was staged in the hall by students of the Theater Arts Department. I arrived when the prologue was just starting. The narrator, a tall man in *ankara* fabric with well kept beards, appeared on stage. He stared outlandishly for a while at a shrine where fire was burning in a clay pot. As if something suddenly struck his mind, he bowed. Taking a few steps closer to the pot, he stopped and nodded in approval and then turned to speak to the viewers.

The gaze of the narrator was complimented by a rhythmic drumming in the background. The sound built up rapidly and dropped to a sustained softness. Then the narrator began to speak:

In this land of the Wanri, crops have yielded
heavily.
The gods have caused the earth to prosper.
Toil is not a foil,
Soil is not oil.
Soil is soil.
Now, mothers make merry.
Fathers make merry.
Children make merry.
Even goats are contented; goats feed on yam peels and are
fattened.
Fowls pick corn grains everywhere in the compound!
Earthworms heap mounds of biomass.
Earth itself makes merry.

The narrator cleared his throat. He took several steps to the left edge of the stage, a few back to the right and remained there. Singing and drumming continued from the background. The narrator continued to speak:

When the gods are so generous to man,
It is because man is not an animal.

It is because man drinks palm-wine with man and with the gods.

A farmer came on stage. His chest was bare, except for an arm of a wrapper running over one of his shoulders from the waist. He held a machete in his right hand. There was a tuber of yam in the left. This farmer was returning from the farm, whistling and nodding with approval at the blessing of his gods. A man and his two wives also emerged from the other end of the stage. They were on their way to salute the gods at the shrine with yams, palm-oil and a fowl, for the blessings. The farmer and the others met. They saluted one another. Then the farmer turned to accompany the others to the shrine.

The narrator continued speaking:

Man is man.
Animal is animal.
Tortoise says to snake; I cannot be bitten!
Drake says to Rooster; I swim in the waters, walk the earth,
And also fly with birds!
Man celebrates with brother in good
And cries with same in bad.
When brother does not join brother to celebrate,
It is because he is diseased in the head.
Otherwise, his spirit is not at rest.
It befits man to struggle.
Yes!
It befits man to make conscious efforts.
To struggle not,
Is to wait for days pregnant with shame.
When man dialogues
with earth
and the gods return sweet for sweat,
He should be merry.
Not to be merry is being sick in the head.

A youth in school uniform entered from the end where the farmer had earlier emerged. He staggered and dragged himself forward with heavy steps. His clothes were stained with blood from several injuries on his body. The farmer beheld the youth from a distance. The youth was his son. He hurried to support him. The youth collapsed and passed out. The farmer began to scream: 'Son! Son!! Son!!!'

The man and his two wives stood, mesmerized by the horror. The two wives suddenly threw down the yams and palm-oil jar, put their hands on their heads. They began to wail and blubber. The scene attracted the townspeople who came in twos and in threes.

The narrator moved a few steps forward, breathed heavily, and continued to speak:

A son that does well in life is the son of all.

But a foolish son belongs only to his mother.

This youth was the only son of the community who was schooling in a university.

Schooling in Ikeja, in a neighbouring town where a university just opened.

Now, blood jets out. Blood. Bloodshed!

The drama continued for at least over half an hour. In the end, the message was very clear. The youth was the only hope of a community that never had a university graduate before. He went to the university to obtain a degree. But at the university, he joined a cult group and lost his life as well as shattered the hopes of many. The play was not only captivating but instructive. The message sank deeply. It reminded me of Mama's advice that I should never engage in such things in the university. I remembered how Mama had spoken to me about this that evening in the village until she began to shed tears. The orientation came to an end towards noon.

A week after, our classes began.

The first lecture we had was with a middle-aged man called Dr. Ayaola. He was a tall, skinny, handsome man, but he walked with a limp on the left leg. When standing straight, from a lateral view, he was almost an 'i.' Ayaola took us in a General Studies course. That morning, the lecture hall was filled. We sat and waited for the lecture that was to begin at 8 o'clock. Ayaola walked in a little after 8. He wrote both his name and the course we would be taking on the blackboard quietly. Most students did not notice his presence as they continued chatting until Ayaola cleared his throat audibly. The noise died out and the class became quiet.

'I suppose my handwriting is visual-friendly... Ahaaah! My name is Ayoala. Dr. Ayo-a-la, if you care so much as to add a title. Usually, I simply prefer Ayoala. You would like to know why. As far as I am concerned, titles are a cheap way the white man bought our conscience. When the white man first came to us, he brought titles along. To our people, if a man had a title, it was a sign that he had come in contact with *Oyibo*. So, Jaja became King Jaja of Opobo. My question is was, Jaja not the king of Opobo? Why did *Oyibo* have to stress it? The *Oyibo* that imported the title culture himself had become 'Lord'. Soon our people began to answer Chief, Prince, Engineer, Barrister and so on. The least of people who could not get titles were offered Mister. Our people cherished this new invention so much that people who traveled to Israel became JPs and to Mecca, Alhajis. A man once begged that if he could not be given any title, at least he should be addressed with the title of 'Late' which is freely given the dead. The truth is our people really never knew if titles were anything reasonable. They simply assumed titles were important because the white man brought them. To me, titles are *Oyibo's* property. I don't care much about them, So I am Ayoala. I will be taking GST 105: African People and their Cultures. You will learn about black magic, colonialism and much more in this course. You have to know who your ancestors were, where they lived, what they lived for, and how they lived. This is a very interesting course and I hope we will have a great time together. Few rules, please: Always come to my class on time. Don't be late. It's 8a.m every Monday, in case you forget, be reminded. I will always be here on time and you have to keep your side of the deal. Rule Number Two: Turn in my assignments. And the last but perhaps most important, you must have at least 95% of attendance to pass this course. You are all adults. I expect you to be attentive when we are discussing these serious issues. There is something I feel compelled to emphasize also: You see, a teacher is like a candle – a good teacher, I mean. The candle burns itself to offer light freely. That is exactly what I will be doing, burning myself to give you light. Hold unto this light. The one with light usually goes by a pit without falling into it. Now, this is very important. If you have a question when I am in class, lift up your hand quietly. You have to cherish the ethics and culture of our togetherness. You are not animals. I will give you the opportunity to talk when appropriate. Do you all get me?'

We chorused a resounding 'Yeees Sir.'

'Does anyone have a question so far?'

The class was quiet, except for the shuffling of feet on the floor and a cautious cough somewhere.

He gazed round, 'Well, I suppose you have no questions. But I have a question for you, and it is pretty serious. Who was the first black man on African soil?'

The hall was quiet.

'Who? Any attempt?'

A skinny girl who wore glasses lifted a hand and stood.

'Young beauty, you think you know? Ahaaah, help us out then!' Ayoala smiled.

'Adam.' The girl said, and then sank back into her seat.

'Adam!' The lecturer exclaimed. 'Adam! Which Adam? I should have loved to know, but you have taken your seat. The man with Eve in the Good Garden? How would you be so sure, Beauty? Anyway, that was a good effort class, let's appreciate her.'

We clapped. Ayoala emphasized that he wasn't satisfied with the answer. So other students stood and made attempts too. A boy said Satan was the first man in Africa. We all laughed. Another student said God. Another said an ape, a kind of ape. We laughed each time an answer was funny or sounded absurd.

Ayoala was pacing the length of the podium. He stopped suddenly, half way and he asked who the first white American in America was. Several students raised their hands. 'Christopher Columbus in 1492,' a student answered. 'George Washington who was the first president of America,' another said. Ayoala smiled again and said he was happy that they could at least mention human names. He said he did not really care who it was that was the first American in America, but wanted us to know that Africa had a lot for us to learn about.

'Africa needs to be studied, and studied indiscriminately in fact. Its people need to be studied, because Africa is amazing.' The man concluded. We applauded.

The skinny girl with glasses lifted her hand again and stood. 'They call black people plantation babies and sugarcane eaters in other parts of the world. Such names make people feel less human! Sir, how does learning about Africa help to change that?'

Ayoala nodded for a while, pacing the stage again. He stopped suddenly and asked the girl her name and then continued, 'First, you will be the class representative for this course. Secondly, I want you to understand something: It is not what you failed to do that has brought you to this point in your life but what you did and what you are still doing. Now, I want you to stop blaming yourself for what you are not doing or what someone else is doing. Don't hate yourself because someone somewhere thinks you are what you are not. Let me relate a beautiful thing that Martin Luther King, Jr. once said. He said that *through your suffering and your willingness to accept blows without retaliating, you have at that moment found yourself working on the conscience of the opponent. You are exposing his moral defences, you are weakening his morale!* I particularly think that Luther said something beautiful! You are beautiful, you know that. If what you are doing does not get you to where you want, get right there and do something! Now, this is enough. Today is only our introductory class and I will not burden you with much. But I would want you all to do something for me. You will write down names of ten black people who got there and did something to change the face of history. It is your homework – ten marks. You will submit that in our next class, first thing. Do not copy from friends. Alright?'

We chorused, 'Yeees Sir.'

'Thank you,' Ayaola said and then left the class.

My love for the university began to grow. I felt a strong urge to attend all my classes and early too. I took all my lectures serious. I would wake up very early, sometimes by 4a.m or at most 5a.m, have my bath and go to class. If I waited till 6a.m, I would sit at the back and not get the lecturer clearly.

I hated sitting at the back of the hall. Students made a lot of noise there. They chewed gum and talked while lectures were going on. Sometimes a boy would lap a girl and one would virtually see the two kissing each other. One day, such a thing happened even in the strangest fashion; I saw a boy run his fingers on a girl's breasts while a lecture was going on! But since the population of our class was so large, it was difficult for a lecturer to notice such things.

People said it was academic freedom. Some sort of freedom this was. I knew what I was here at the university for. I was totally prepared to face my studies in earnest.

I returned to the hostel, into our noisy room. A 200-level student, Charles, was sleeping on his bed under my bunk. He snored lightly and chewed his tongue in his sleep. He always did that, sleep-eating his tongue. Then he would wake up to find that saliva had threaded a yellowish dry layer on his cheek. Charles was the kind that could sleep all day and night, and still look sleepy even when he was awake. This boy would sometimes even miss his classes due to sleep. I was often baffled at how he managed to sleep despite the noise that was always made in our room by our roommates.

My sixteen co-habitants were in the room such that it warmed under our collective breaths. Officially, this hostel room was allocated to four of us. But my three original roommates had taken in friends who had no allocation from the school and could not afford to pay for housing. The unofficial room members whom we called squatters were usually the loudest noise makers.

Whenever an argument erupted in the room, it went tense- like now when I returned from class. The argument was about European football, particularly the Champions' League.

I dropped my books on my bunk, picked a tuber of yam from the cupboard and began to peel it. We cooked our meals ourselves because our school fees did not cover provision of food by the school.

After setting the yam on fire to boil, I hurried to the bathroom to bath. The shower was running today. Most times, it did not. When I returned to the room, the yam was done. I brought the pot down from the kerosene stove and put the flame out. I could not wait for the yam to cool before I would eat. I was pretty hungry.

Muhammad, the most senior student in the room whom we called 'FYB' or Final Year Brother, was lying on his bunk beside the window. FYB was a nice person. He would always keep food for me if he cooked in my absence, so I always invited him to join me when eating.

'FYB, join me let's eat', I said keeping the pot of yam on the floor.

He took a seat and joined me. Soon, the other roommates came uninvited and crowded the food, fast munching pieces of the yam like a battalion of hungry ants. In the end, I barely ate two pieces before the yam was wiped out from the pot. I went for a cup of water and retired to bed while the argument resumed. It was a while before I drifted into sleep.

The intensity of the argument in the room woke me up minutes later. I looked at the time. It was past 2p.m. The room being impossible to stay in, I picked a book and left. I had no particular destination in mind at first but ended up going to the lecture hall.

The lecture halls were almost empty and quiet, except for bats hissing in the roofs. I sat and began to read, initially with sleepy eyes, until 6p.m when several students started arriving. Now, the hostel room must be less noisy, I thought then left the lecture hall and returned to the hostel. When I got to the room, FYB was reading in his corner. Fakun, a 300level student of Economics, was sleeping on his up-bunk. The rest were out. I greeted FYB, prepared and took a cup of *gari*, then I prayed and slept.

The next afternoon, thoughts of Mama kept lingering in my mind. I was worried about her. Was the pain in her chest getting any better, or worse? How was she coping with farm work without my assistance?

Even though Mama was a strong woman, I feared that it was too hard for her to go on without help.

There was something that amazed me about Mama, something I could not discuss generally: I had never seen Mama stand with a man and talk in a romantic manner. Not even for once had a suitor come to see her in my entire growing years. She was her own woman. As I walked back to the hostels, I made up my mind that I would make her proud. Since that woman had stood strong for me almost all alone, then I was going to give her reasons to be proud of me. I was going to do anything within acceptable limits to obtain good grades in school. When I graduated with flying colours, she would reap fulfillment.

But why did Mama not abort the pregnancy which brought me forth when the circumstances surrounding it were so painful and brought her so much shame? I had asked myself this question again and again without getting answers.

I got into my room, dropped my notebooks on my bed, and took off my *Safari*. I was hungry and I soaked *gari*. When I began to take it, FYB called me and offered me a plate of white rice with stew.

There had been power outage this afternoon. The ceiling fan was idle and the room was very hot. As I ate, a student with a lame leg, who stayed in a room next to ours came in. He stood behind me, saying nothing. I didn't bother to talk to him either. He stood there for a while staring at me, then he hissed and turned, limping as he went. The boy was troublesome; his disability was not worth any sympathy. He was like a possessed person.

Somehow, I could not stop worrying about mother. But I also realized her strength and dwelt on it. 'Life has a way of shaping us as people', I concluded. Maybe, hers was meant to be a tough journey. I hoped that when I graduated from the university, I would make things easier for her. Somehow, I felt the need for her to get a man, a good man, and marry. I felt the compulsion to talk to her about this. The thought obsessed and tormented me.

I decided to get a novel and read. Just anything that would take my mind off the thought.

I met FYB and requested for a novel and he gave me a volume of Terry Waite's poignant self-portrait, *Taken on Trust*. The book was voluminous but I decided to start reading it.

In the book, Mr. Waite, a fine character, was a 6 foot tall and robust-bodied Sassenach who was involved in a rescue mission for captives held in the Middle-East country town of Beirut. Waite had gone round planet earth over and over to reinstitute peace, and had particularly worked in Africa with missionaries with a fever of love. In Uganda, he met a man with a lion's mind, Idi Amin. Desmond Tutu in Black and White South Africa was a Nobel peace prize winner and Waite's friend. Waite was also in Ghana and Nigeria. The man, the peace worker, went to Beirut to hunt for peace. That was where he was taken captive. For 1, 763 days, Terry was behind a prison wall in Beirut in total solitude. Each day, he wrote his novel in his head with a fervent spirit. No pen. No book. He just wrote in the head. Death came but he held his breath against it.

Somehow, the story gave me the assurance that at the end of every tunnel, there is light. No prison is forever locked. As I read the book, some other fine books which I had read earlier such as Pever X's *Cat Eyes*, Isidore Okpewho's *The Last Duty*, and Chinua Achebe's *Ant-Hills of the Savannah* came to mind.

I began to write my own book in my head that day. I was not sure of what title I would give my book, but I started writing anyway.

I knew from that day that one day I would make Mama proud.

There was power failure again. It was dawn, and cold. I had lit a half-used candle in the middle of the night to read but it flickered and fizzled out.

Mosquitoes had made it difficult to sleep throughout the night. It was when dawn approached that I finally began to sleep. I slept until it was almost 7 a.m.

Bt 7, classes were almost about to start already. I jumped out of bed and into the bathroom, took my bath, dressed and hurried to class. Unfortunately, all the front seats were already occupied by the time I arrived. I was lucky to escape a little drizzling outside the hall. Soon, it turned to rain. Thunder echoed sporadically but the sun was still shinning. The rain continued until it was almost 9 a.m. We sat, waiting for a lecturer. While waiting, a student was leading the class in morning devotion. I joined as we sang praises.

In the midst of the ongoing praises, a young man who sat on my left with a girl was running his fingers on her laps. They would pause laugh and continue. As distracting as they were, when the devotion ended, I began to do a history assignment which was due for submission the next morning.

A handsome young man called Udaka came and spoke to the girl who was with the guy. Udaka's voice rose in anger as he spoke. I suspected she was his girlfriend in the arms of another man. After some exchanges, Udaka turned and walked out of the hall hard-faced.

Minutes later, when I looked up, I saw Udaka returning from the main door of the hall. I knew from his grimace that trouble was brewing. But I knew that he would not start a fight. Fighting was against the school rules. It attracted outright expulsion and students usually avoided it. But in the hostels, sometimes, students would fight- especially if they were only two in a closet. They would lock themselves in a room and fight their teeth out. If anyone barged in on them, they would claim they were playing.

Udaka stopped in front of the couple and pulled a pistol from under his shirt. My nostrils flared as he lifted the gun, pointing it straight at the young man whose hand was still on the girl's lap. Like a scene in an action movie, the pistol popped, *kpaaaa*!

That was the last thing I saw. I passed out, apparently.

When I recovered and could see again, I was on the floor, shivering. I lost clear vision for some minutes. The explosion of the gun was so loud it affected my hearing for a while. It was the first time I had ever heard a live gunshot. I looked at the young man who had been shot, lying on the floor. His forehead was pierced and blood was gushing out. The girl had collapsed in shock too. Three of us were on the floor.

I could have heard voices of students running out of the hall in fear. Screams rent the air. When I could stand, the hall was completely deserted. My head hung heavy as if under a weight. I began to toddle to the door where some of my classmates stood peeping into the hall.

Outside the lecture hall, my heart continued to thump. The image of the murdered student was on my mind. Few students came and met me. They wanted to know what had happened. Soon, many more came so that I turned a spectacle. My *safari* had caught dirt from the floor. I dusted it with the back of my hand as I walked away to the shade at a tree. The lecture hall was surrounded by trees, some of which had metal-chairs fastened to the ground, where students relaxed. This gave the place the name 'Relaxation Park.' It was still damp outside the hall as rain drops were still on the seats. I wiped the seat and sat staring towards the library. It was 10:28 a.m.

I could see two security operatives run into the hall. Soon, they brought out the girl whose friend was shot. She had fainted. The crowd hurried to catch a glimpse of her. One of the security men was fanning her with a book while the other was trying to keep the spectators away. About an hour later, it occurred to me that I had left my books in the hall on the desk. I got up and began to walk to the hall. As I got to the door, a truck pulled over and 4 policemen jumped into the hall.

One of the policemen, a very dramatic man with crude swiftness, had a rifle while his other colleagues had batons. The rifle man positioned himself with obdurate agility. One could see that this man was ready to shoot a housefly if it passed the wrong way at such a time.

The man with the rifle came out from the hall almost immediately and began to talk on a phone, 'Oga.. Oga… yes sir…yes sir,' He was reporting to his superior.

About forty minutes later another truck pulled up in front of the lecture hall. Two policemen came out from the truck alongside the Dean of Students' Affairs, Dr. Eugene Akaki. Dr. Akaki and the policemen entered into the hall. We followed. As we approached the corpse, I noticed the lips had slackened and a film of yellowish saliva bubbled down the jaw while the hole in the head still dripped blood.

A photographer was invited into the hall. He and Dr. Akaki

conferred briefly then he turned to the corpse and began to click away with his camera from different angles. After the shots, the corpse was wrapped in a black cloth and hauled into the first truck. We followed outside the hall where the Dean explained that everything was under control. The police were investigating the incident and the 'perpetrators' would be 'brought to book,' he concluded.

Dr. Akaki informed us that senate of the university was aware of the activities of cultists on campus and steps were being taken to bring the menace to a permanent end.

We watched the two trucks whirl off, generating massive smoke. As I stood staring at the departing trucks, someone's hand rested calmly on my shoulder. I turned to look. To my surprise it was Aker, my friend from primary school! He stood here smiling at me. 'Woooooo! Is this a dream?' I asked, rubbing my eyes repeatedly.

Since we left the primary school in Akan, I had not seen Aker. While I had left for Mbaikyo for my secondary education, Aker had gone to school in Makurdi where his elder sister was married. Tabi had told me that she had seen him a couple of times in a church there. Seeing him her in IBRU was like a miracle.

Life was going to take a sudden twist for me, getting a lot more interesting. I supposed.

For two days, tap water had not run in the hostels. It was frustrating.

This was not the first time water supply had ceased for days. There was a week, the entire week, we hadn't any water. When one visited the toilet, one would find so much feces piled in there such that it was impossible to use the toilets. Students had started littering the bushes around the hostels with excreta.

The first semester exams were just a week away. The Students Union President came and addressed us in our hostel. He called us all out and began to assure us that he was meeting with the Vice Chancellor that evening. He would tell the Vice Chancellor it was unacceptable for students to live without water on campus. We applauded the decision. Such a step was important for us. Water was not to be played with like light. When light failed, we used candles. But without water, we could do nothing.

So we waited for the Students Union President to meet with the Vice Chancellor and tell us the result.

All day, as I idled around in the hostel, thoughts of the murdered student kept flashing through my mind.

By evening, the heat in the rooms had increased with mosquitoes tormenting us as well. I lay on my bunk and picked up *Taken on Trust* again, using candlelight to read it. Reading would distract me from thoughts of the student murdered in my class today.

Although the Waite story was intriguing, I now read it with exertion; a line twice or even trice. I just couldn't get past the murder.

Lame Leg came into our room. This time, he came and asked about his missing clothes which he had spread outside in front of his room on a line. I told him I never saw them. For a while, he blabbed that he would use a certain powerful medicine which he acquired from his father who was a *juju* man, and the student who stole the items would run mad. Then he hissed and left the room. I followed him with my eyes to the door.

Lame Leg went out and almost immediately, Aker came in.

'Aondokaa Fada!' My friend saluted when he came to my bunk.

'Aker Fada!' I saluted calmly, smiling. The Electrical Engineering student had not changed from the little boy I had known back in the primary school at Akan. He was same funny Aker.

I got off the bed and offered him a seat, but he declined. The heat in the room was intense and he wanted us to go to the Students Union Podium in front of the hostels. We left the room.

Soon, a crescent moon began to emerge in the sky.

'How did your day go?' Aker asked when we had sat at the podium.

'Appalling'. I replied.

An easy smile swept across the oblong face. Aker had that intriguing smile that accompanied his soft words.

We began to discuss the murder.

'These churchmen are quite ruthless,' he observed.

'You mean people from the church?'

'Cultists, I mean. They use the name "churchmen" to masquerade their identity.'

'Sorry?' I asked.

'You know that if the school finds out a student is a cultist, the student is withdrawn immediately?'

'We were informed during the orientation ceremony.' I said.

He nodded in approval, 'Yet, unfortunately there are several students involved. Perhaps, lecturers too! Cultists usually refer to students who do not accept to become a part of them as "Jews", which means the non-members have roots in godliness and do not understand their actions.'

'Really! But why do people get involved in cultism?' I wondered.

He smiled, 'Bad influence maybe,' Aker said.

'Influence? Why? I mean, how?'

Aker cleared his throat, 'An empty head, it is said, is nothing but load to the neck. It doesn't matter the size of that head. Empty heads are easily filled with anything and easily influenced. It's like people who do not have a mind of their own, like the tale about a bull that kept pulling the wagon in fear of the club, without a mind of its own. I once sat, and in the depth of my imaginations, considered cultism as a graveyard; I discovered that in the graves, there is a defeated crowd, people who are only a shadow of themselves. People who could have been professors, governors, doctors, engineers, lawyers, and celebrities, heroes and heroines who will not see the day of their success come. Their names will never be heard or remembered. In their graves, they lie with dried lips, frustrated with bitterness on their faces. These are the most pitiable of humans! Truly, each individual must map a road for himself with his own hands, and carve a shoe for his feet. That's it. That is the way that leads to the top with sustained happiness. We young people must become more visionary, and have a clear sense of direction and definiteness of purpose. We must become proactive and have positive minds of our own, I mean. It's vital.'

'Yeah,' I agreed.

'Youths must recognize that youthfulness is an opportunity, a wonderful one. And the world is eager to feel our positive impact. This is important! Life has three key stages; childhood, youth, and old age. In childhood, children present potentials, in youth young people should express their potentials, and in old age people should create legacies. As youths, we should not embrace such madness as campus cultism so gladly! The Tiv say, even a mad man knows exactly when it is a market day. Is it not so?'

I nodded in total agreement.

'The recognition of this fact should shield you from bad influence, from campus cultism. And this has to be a deliberate decision'.

'You mean campus cultists suffer from identity crises?' I asked.

'Exactly! You see, Aondoakaa, when you look at history, great people were ordinary people with great positive minds. No one gets to the top in life as a second class feeble mind. You get me?'

I nodded.

'Cultism, so far as I know, is a graveyard. And I reject it,' Aker said in a soft but firm voice.

'You speak like the professor who came to school the other day to give an inaugural lecture.'

'You mean Jibo?'

I nodded, 'They say that the man went to *Oyibo* country and performed better than the *Oyibos* in learning their own secrets!' I continued. 'He was condemning tribal violence that day when he said, "We have our differences, but we can't give away our brotherliness. It is like saying: The Tiv, that terrible tribe of rat eaters! They eat bush rats! But that's not all; they also eat snakes, snails, and toads too! But we all eat one thing or another as a matter of fact, each of us from one tribe to the other!'

'Building a happy, united and great nation is a collective effort; I agree with the professor completely,' Aker said.

I had made up my mind even when I was in the village that, once on campus, I was headed for success and would avoid any evil involvements. Nothing was capable of getting me involved with such vices as cultism, I wanted to assure my friend, but instead I nodded again and smiled to myself. He gazed at me intently. In the moonlight, his eyes sank into their sockets. Probably, he was wondering if he was making any sense.

A mosquito buzzed around my ear. I slapped it away, at the same time saluting FYB as walked past us and headed towards the lecture halls with a number of books in his hand. The hostel was very noisy, more so because there was no light and many students were lazing around.

'You are here for a purpose. Achieve it!' Aker continued. We continued speaking until light was eventually restored minutes to midnight. I accompanied Aker to the gate of my hostel and he promised to take me to his room the next day.

I returned to my room and slept.

The next morning, I was woken by students beating broken buckets, metallic plates, used milk tins, and chanting towards the Students Union podium. I looked through the window and saw several students singing on top of their voices. Girls from the two female hostels were there too. I climbed out of my bunk, wore a Danshiki and stepped out of the hostel building to have a better view of what was happening.

As the students got to the podium, they began to sing:

'We no go gree! We
no go gree!! Water
no dey!
'Light no dey!
Tuition too much!
We no go gree!
'We no go gree -o!
We no go gree!!'

The voices echoed from the walls of the hostels. Soon, I realized there were several groups going around. One group headed to the Coca Cola Park. When that group got there, they began to block the road with logs of wood and palm-fronds. Close to the library, another group had blocked the road there and also started a fire with an old car-tyre. The burning tyres gave off thick black smoke in the air. These students were dancing round the fires, singing loudly, 'We no go gree... No water! No school! No light, no school..!' Looking towards the Coca-Cola Park now, I saw another group chanting towards the administrative block.

FYB came and stood beside me at the door.

'Two years ago, we had a similar situation and school was shut down. Oh, not again.' He said, shaking his head as I looked at him quietly. For a final year student who had spent two extra years for a course of four years due to truncated semesters, I could see how much he wanted to write his exams and graduate. Personally, I was also eager to start my exams.

Presently, the Students Union President came to the podium and FYB suggested that we go and listen. Soon, the president was crowded as he stood head-above-the-crowd on the podium and began to shoot his fist in the air as though punching it. Each time he shot his fist, he shouted, 'Greatest IBRU students!' And the students responded, 'Great!' When he had gotten the attention of those present, he began to speak. When he wanted to make a point, he would say, 'I want to articulate!' And the students would respond, 'Articulate!' At other times, he would say 'I want to quote!' or 'I want to say!'

I watched with interest but my lips would not open in solidarity.

'Greatest IBRU students, I want to say!' The president cried.

'Say!'

'My fellow students, exams are only a week away and I am sure everyone here is aware of this. It is however very unfortunate that living conditions on campus have worsened in these last weeks. There has been very epileptic power supply in the past week, more terrible than ever! There is no water at all! The toilets are messed up since it has become impossible to flush them. We are living like a bunch of animals. And how would anyone expect us to do well in exams under these poor conditions? Yet that is what the school is expecting of us. It's unfair! Fellow students, I have seen our plight and will ensure that the correct thing is done before any exams begin, or shall we continue like this?'

'Noooooooo!' The crowd replied.

'We are not animals, we are humans and as a matter of fact the future of our country is in our hands. We can't continue like this my fellow students!'

'Noooooooo!' The crowd shouted.

'Very well,' the president continued. 'I want us to return to our hostels and remain peaceful. I, your president, will see this matter to its conclusion, in your best interest. Meanwhile, I have directed officials of the union to go to all classes and lock them up to shut down academic activities'.

He received cheerful applause as he climbed down the podium.

As we returned to the hostels, the rooms became even more noisy. Classes were locked up by the Students Union so most of the students were in the hostels. I climbed onto my bunk and lay down.

My roommates returned to the room and began to debate on the situation, expressing various opinions.

An hour had passed when Charles, my sleeping-all-day-and-all-night roommate, returned from hostel Block A and said he had seen a circular that school was shutdown. We were to vacate the hostels immediately, before noon. Already, armed policemen were waiting at the school gate to come in by noon, to chase out students from the hostels.

### St. Winifred, Akan 

The police drove into the school in truck-loads. They were carrying guns and *koboko*s whips. All of them in their khakis stormed our rooms, ordered us out. It was past 11 a.m. 'School is shut down and you are to vacate immediately. You pose a major security threat,' one of the policemen who came into our room said. When the police officers saw that we were putting our luggage together hurriedly in preparation to leave, they left for Lame Leg's room next door.

I had just gathered my belongings into my *Ghana-must-go* bag. While taking the bag out of the room, I heard a gunshot. It was fired at the Students Union Podium. My roommates all ran out of the room. It was a frightening sound.

From the door, I looked in the direction of the blast. I could see a police officer struggling over a rifle with a student near the podium. The officer who hung the rifle across his chest with a gun-belt held the student firmly by the trousers. The student was struggling to disarm him of the gun. Soon, the student broke away. He began to run towards the school library where a burnt car-tyre was still sending diminutive smoke into the air.

Two policemen chased the student. Soon, a number of students who came out from the hostels followed. Whether the students were helping the police officer in chasing the student or going after the police officer, I was not sure. But after a while, we heard another gunshot. That was when I realized that what was going on was beyond my estimation. Standing there was no longer safe. I ran into the room, picked my *Ghana-must-go* bag and ran out. Soon, I was heading towards the Coca Cola Park, to the mini-campus.

I continued running with the bag on my head, passing several other students who were dragging their luggage, until I got to the bus-stop at the school gate. The bus-stop was already crowded with students who were waiting for buses. There were no buses. It wasn't long after I brought the bag down from my head that I heard another gunshot from the hostels. Waiting there at the bus-stop too became risky. I felt it was more reasonable to trek out of the school. Possibly, I would stop a bus which was coming into school. Sometimes, buses came half empty from town. But somehow, I still stood there. A student who had just come to the bus stop informed us that some students and the police were engaged in a fight. 'A policeman is killed. Students are stoning the police, chasing them away'.

I left the bus-stop, my bag balanced on my head, and headed for the school gate hurriedly. As I approached the gate, I saw the signboard with the inscription, "WELCOME TO UNIVERSITY OF IBRU – The Pace Setting University of the Country" again. The inscription got me wondering that if IBRU was indeed a pace-setting institution in the country, yet things were so bad here, what were the other universities like?

I passed by the school gate where the two school security guards sat on a bench, discussing. I saluted the men and continued on my way some kilometers down the road. Eventually, I saw a bus carrying firewood; it was going to town. Apart from the wood, the driver had just a passenger in front, a middle aged lady. I waved at them so vigorously that after passing me, they went ahead a while and stopped.

Women from town came to the university sometimes to cut down trees and take them to town to sell as firewood. It was one of the vehicles conveying such wood that I joined. As we drove away, we saw a truck loaded with armed policemen on their way to school.

The firewood bus arrived a roundabout in town close to the motor park where two *Yellow Fever* traffic wardens stood directing vehicles. Traffic was dense. Market women crowded at the shoulder of the road selling items of various sorts: vegetables, grains, palm-oil, fish and other things.

A man who sold native medicine was advertising the products; 'Buy native medicine. Na em better pass *Oyibo* medicine because native medicine na herbs. Goat de eat only herb, na em make goat no de sick! Buy medicine from here. E de cure belle palaver, de cure headache, de cure any woman or man infection wey *Oyibo* de call sexually transmitted disease. Na herb good for your body'.

A *Mei-ruwa,* a water vendor, was pushing water in a truck across the road. Even the town had been hit by the water scarcity. The bus came to a stop by the side of the narrow road near the pack and I alighted; taking my bag along. I began to trace my way through the crowd gradually until I got to the motor-park.

At the park, I was lucky to meet the last saloon car for Mbaikyo. Since Urokpa was a mega city, it was easier to get vehicles at late hours of the day heading for Mbaikyo than when one was coming from Mbaikyo to Urokpa. I got there when it had just one vacant seat left. I paid and boarded the vehicle. The driver was a skinny man probably in his fifties with unkempt beard. He started the car, it made a loud noise and smoked heavily before he engaged the gear and the car began to roll with a vigorous vibration. But in the end, we had a safe trip to Mbaikyo.

I got to Akan the next day. Mama was in her hut when I arrived. I knocked at her door gently, 'Who is it?' She asked.

'Aondoakaa,' I replied.

Mama came out and hugged me tightly.

'I say Obasanjo is a coward and a dim-witted element of indefinable futility! Summit of compound inanity! Meaningless arrogant quantity of foolishness! That is who he is! He thinks he is somebody? He is a nobody! Obasanjo thinks he is somebody? I ask! Very well then! Very well! The coward cannot keep withholding my hard-earned pension benefits! Say who die! I swear, I will shoot him in the nyash!' The man continued his tirade as he sat on a wooden bench, digging his index finger into his nostril. His bicycle lay upside-down as he ran the back wheel, greasing the chain.

Despite his little exposure to formal education, Eliza's husband always used exotic vocabulary that would give one the impression that he was well schooled. Sometimes, I wondered how he was able to acquire those words. When he spoke in local meetings or at the beer joint with his friends, people would say he had lost his mind.

Adu, his son, came from his mother's kitchen where he had gone to get a piece of roasted yam. He went and sat under the cashew tree and began to play. The boy had only a pair of dirty and torn pants on. Eliza, his mother, was in her kitchen. She was just recovering from a miscarriage. Mama said her husband had punched the foetus out during one of their arguments.

'I say Obasanjo is a rascal! A rogue! In fact, Obasanjo is an animal!' The man lifted his eyes and regarded his playing son briefly. He seemed to be having more of an internal dialogue, muttering words silently. He got up suddenly, as though his annoyance had filled his heart to the brim. He ran the back tyre of the bicycle one more time and then turned it upright. He rang the bell, his right hand grasping the horn of the bicycle firmly. He then pushed the bicycle to the cashew tree, rested it against the tree and warned his son not to play around it. As he walked into their hut, his wife came out, got some water in a little green bowl from a big metallic basin by the door and returned into the kitchen.

In a while, the man came out from the hut with a white

sleeveless shirt on and a wrapper round his waist firmly knotted in front. He went to his bicycle and pulled it from where it lay. He placed his left leg on the left pedal and pushed with his right for a while until the bicycle could sustain itself in motion, then he climbed.

His son called, 'Baba, buy *kwesi*…!'

The man seemed not to get the boy very clearly but he waved as he rode down towards the banana plantation at the back of my mother's hut. He disappeared behind the thin bush-path.

The sun shone steadily into a bright day. One of Eliza's goats came to the door of Mama's hut and began to eat a tuber of yam that Mama kept against the wall. I picked a stone and drove the animal away. It wandered in the compound for a while and returned to the tuber again.

Mama came out of the hut and drove the goat away. She picked the yam and took it into her kitchen.

Mama's left breast had swollen a little with the lump, and she complained that an object was still moving in there. So I insisted that we go to the clinic at the primary school for a checkup. But she was adamant; she said she would be okay, at least the pawpaw roots and *egwu* leaves she squeezed in Holy Water and took every morning were beginning to bring some relief to her. She had even added some ginger roots and potato leaves to the mixture so that it thickened into a green gel.

'Mama, I think it is important that you be checked at the clinic.'

'I will be fine…'

'At the clinic you will at least know what keeps moving in the breast.'

'Son, I know what it is; blood. It is blood.'

I stared at Mama for a while. She had emaciated.

'Blood moves in every living human; people don't know when their blood runs…'

'Look, son, I know what you mean. And I would go to the clinic. But you know I don't have the money now. The little I have, I am keeping for your transport fare, when your school calls… Yet I have to look for more at the moment.'

I stared at her for a while and she stared back. Then, I looked away and cleared my throat.

'Mama, how is Eliza doing? I mean, you said she lost her pregnancy...'

'Initially, it was difficult for her. Sometimes, I would even have to help her to the toilet. It was that terrible. But she is much better now. At least she is able to make *luam* for the little boy.' Mama turned and regarded the playing Adu briefly.

'He is growing so fast,' I said.

'He eats a lot.'

'He is just a copy of the father... Mama, look at the nose; how it twists into an inverted W like the father's.'

Mama smiled, 'Yet, he keeps insulting his wife that the boy looks like a woman.'

'Has he lost his eyes?'

Mother smiled again, 'Sometimes he says he has... There was this day when he was eating some food under the cashew tree in the evening when a friend of his came around. The man kept on eating without inviting the friend to join him. His friend stood there and watched as the man ate until he could no longer hold his peace. He decided to join in the meal uninvited. That was when the man said that he saw his friend. I laughed.'

'That was terrible,' I said, smiling.

'He does funny things these days... You know, age is telling on him.'

Eliza came out from the kitchen and walked across to her hut.

'Mama, I should go and greet Eliza...'

'Oh yes! It is good you greet her.'

I walked to the door of Eliza's hut and knocked gently. There was no response. I knocked again.

'Who is it?' Eliza asked eventually.

'Aondoakaa...' I replied.

'Come in.'

I pushed the door carefully and entered, leaving it ajar. The room was dark but I could see the figure of the woman as she sat on her bed. After a while, my eyes became accustomed to the darkness so I could see well. A piece of wrapper covered her from the chest down to the thighs.

I saw a little wooden stool on the floor and made for it when the woman called, 'Aondoakaa, come and sit here on the bed.'

'I am fine here,' I said

'My whole waist burns with pain…' she beckoned again. 'Come press the pain out.' She turned and lay, stretching her full length on the bed, then she groaned.

'Are you taking medication at all?' I asked.

'Yes, *Missu*. I am taking *Missu*. It is potato roots that I soak in a solution of goat-urine overnight. I am told it helps…'

'*Yesu krestu*!' I exclaimed. 'Is that the medication?'

She groaned again, 'Come please…'

I went to the bed quickly and sat on the edge. The woman groaned again. Moved by her groans, I impulsively reached for her waist and touched it carefully. She rolled in bed slowly and faced me. Now, the piece of wrapper fell off from her chest so that one of her breasts was out.

'The pain is here,' her hand touched mine and drew it leisurely to her thigh.

'Eliza…'

'The pain is in here…'

'Eliza, please…'

'It pains…'

The woman started again as her fingers quickly sought my sex organ.

I cannot swear that I did not feel the wetness of the woman's crotch with my fingers. And I am ashamed to confess, but it is true that my heart yielded quickly to the desire.

'Eliza, we cannot…'

'Aondoakaa, please…'

The door opened and Adu entered and called out to his mother, telling her he was hungry. When the boy saw me there, he stopped and stared quizzically. But I realized that he was only trying to make out the silhouettes as his eyes adjusted to the darkness in the room. My hand retracted from the woman's thighs swiftly.

'Uncle,' the boy called me finally when he had made out my image. 'I am hungry,' he said.

'Go outside, I will come and give you food.' Eliza said weakly to her son.

The boy stared for a while before he turned and disappeared at the door.

I got up. Eliza's hand made for mine swiftly.

'Come. Aondoakaa, don't go… Adu just had food a while ago. He is only disturbing.'

I cleared my throat, adjusted my trousers, and walked out of the room. When I came out, I saw the boy running after goats towards the cashew tree. He was actually chasing them away from eating the corn plants that were growing near the cashew tree. Mama came out from her kitchen which she recently built and walked to the hut.

I joined Mama in the hut. 'Have you greeted Eliza?' she asked.

'I have. I also wish to check on Aker and see if he has returned to the village. As I left the hut, Mama cautioned, 'Don't come back very late. The village is no longer safe for going around in the night.'

'I will come back early enough,' I assured her and was off.

That evening, when I returned, Mama and I sat in the room late into the night talking when a knock came from the door and we heard someone panting in fear. I asked who it was. Eliza's voice came through feverishly. I got up and opened the door. She entered quickly and stood in the room, breathing unsteadily. Mama asked what the matter was. 'An owl is hooting on top of our roof. The bird has been hooting there for more than an hour. My husband is not back yet,' Eliza said. Mama and I replied that we had heard the owl too but we thought it was coming from somewhere else. Mama asked me to go and bring Adu.

Sometimes, evil spirits went around at night. A hooting owl over one's roof particularly, was not welcome in our village. We became anxious. Eliza's husband had stayed out unusually late. No matter where he went to, the man always came back before Eliza slept. I went to the hut and brought the sleeping child. We all slept in Mama's hut.

The next morning, we were awakened by the wailing of neighbours who came gathering in the church compound. Neighbours were going to their farms early that morning when they found Eliza's husband's body by the rivulet at the back of the church where I had heard water gurgling when Mama first took me to my primary school. A little bush path led to it with a narrow tree-trunk bridge across. The man's bicycle was found hanging upside-down, over the bridge. His lifeless body lay under the clear water. When they brought the body out, it was said that it still oozed of alcohol.

## *University of IBRU, Urokpa-West* 

Eliza came and stood by the door. She was carrying Adu her son against her bosom. My mother was inside the hut. She had just returned from Benediction that evening. Adu breathed like an ailing kitten; his ribs rose and fell heavily.

'He has been crying for food since morning,' Eliza told my mother, 'and there is no food left in the house.' She must have remembered her man again as tears rolled down her cheeks. 'I myself have not eaten anything since morning,' she sniffed.

Mama opened the door wider. She asked her in. Eliza put Adu down and pulled him by the finger into the hut. They stayed in the hut for a while before the boy came out, skipping jubilantly to the cashew tree. Eliza also came out licking the fingers of her left hand as she walked to her hut. Each evening since Eliza's husband died, Mama kept some food for her to eat with her child. Mama would always refer to the food as "a small thing," but it was usually a bowl-full. And Eliza always waited for it.

Eliza was wiping her hands on her wrapper as she entered her hut.

'Are you still travelling tomorrow. Or, have you changed your mind?' Mama asked when I came into the room.

'Yes Mama, I'll be travelling. But I told you earlier that exams will start by Tuesday.'

'Oh, I remember… And today is Sunday?'

'Yes Mama, it's Sunday.'

She sat in her thoughts for a while. 'Your food is beside the water jar behind my bed', she said finally.

'Thank you Mama', I said, dished an encouraging smile.

'Now that Tabi has given you a phone, we can talk to you frequently to know your situation in school,' Mama said. I simply nodded. Even though Mama had no phone, it was easy for her to reach me through Tabi from Makurdi. She would send her messages through Father Gregory when the priest was attending a meeting there.

The smoke from the lantern in the hut choked me. I sneezed. When I started eating the food, mother slept off. She went to bed early that evening. After the food, I went to bed too. The next morning, I woke early, at about quarter past four. Before I left for Urokpa-West, I warmed the leftover cassava soup and *luam* and ate it for breakfast. It was so early that Eliza was not yet awake.

I arrived school that evening and went to my room. The room was so noisy when I got in. With the exception of FYB, all my roommates had resumed and were arguing as usual. But this time, it wasn't an argument about football. It was something different. The school administration had advised all students to buy rechargeable lanterns.

The university administration said the university could no longer guarantee that electricity would be available to students always. And the university senate, in its infinite wisdom, regretted such a thing. Or, so they said. As my roommates debated on the issue, someone sought to know what the position of the students' union on the matter was.

'The story is going around that while students were away, the Vice Chancellor invited those SU boys to his lodge. He slaughtered a cow for them. The SU president is rumoured to have taken money from the VC too. Can the SU say anything now?' one of my roommates said.

I was already so exhausted. Listening to the arguments was even more exhausting. I made my bed and went to sleep.

The next morning, around 5a.m, I went to the bathroom. As I approached the room, I heard the showers running. The lights in the bathroom were off, but light from the corridor shone through the windows. The place was dim. I could make out two figures under the running showers. A young man was making love to another. I stood and watched for a while as he pushed from behind into the other who was grunting. It was almost frightening to stand and watch. So, I turned quietly and returned to my room.

Many terrible things were going on on campus. The place where I had supposed our character would be shaped was also fast becoming a hub for evil. I had seen a piece of condom that was filled with semen the other day when I was going to the library in the morning. I thought that was worth a concern. But to see men making love to each other was frightening.

From this day, the distressing sight would remain in my head.

I returned to my room and lay on my bed, staring at the rotating ceiling fan as it made a *twiki-twiki* noise. All I could see was the two lover men. My roommates were still sleeping.

I had more important things to worry about. My first examination paper for the semester was that evening, at 3p.m. That began to bother me. The academic calendar had been readjusted such that after the examinations, we would continue with the second semester straight away. I had assured Mama during the vacation that I would do well in the exams. And I meant it. I was going to be committed to it.

This evening, Dr Ayaola was the invigilator for the paper. As the man passed the question papers around, he warned us not to open or read them until he had instructed us to do so. But as soon as the man shared the question papers and answer booklets on our row and went to the next, some students began to peep and discuss the questions with each other. When I was handed the question paper, my mind went straight to my commitment to Mama. I remembered how much she was going through back in Akan for me to become a graduate. My resolve to do well in the examinations strengthened.

When Dr. Ayaola gave the permission for us to start, I prayed briefly and opened my question paper. At first, fear gripped me. It appeared I knew nothing by the time I read through the question paper from beginning to end. I lay back in the chair and let my eyes wander around the ceiling. After a while, I prayed again.

Beside me, a lady drew out a piece of paper carefully folded from her pants and began to copy from it. She had prepared answers on the paper already. Her eyes locked with mine for a moment before she withdrew and continued to copy the answers. Dr Ayaola was standing not too far from the cheating girl. But she went on unnoticed. She was not the only one copying answers from pieces of paper that way anyway. There were several others too.

That moment, I wished I had brought into the exam hall pieces of paper with answers copied on them too. But Mama's words came to my mind loudly, 'To make a difference, be different!'

I turned to the question paper and read again. This time, I noticed that I could actually attempt the questions. They were things I had read. I picked my pen and began to answer the questions.

Towards the end of the exam that evening, a tall dark man came to the hall and asked of 'Aondoakaa'. I identified myself. He said I was to see the head of my department the next morning by 8:00 o'clock without fail. When I left the exam hall and returned to the hostel, I wondered what I had to see the HOD for.

By 8:00 a.m the next day, I was at the HOD's office. The man had not come to work yet, but his secretary said it wasn't going to be long before he arrived. So I sat and waited.

The HOD, Professor Okoro Ebube, came in about fifteen minutes later. The secretary welcomed him and took his bag into his office. Shortly, she came out and told me the man was ready to see me. I went to the door, knocked, pushed and entered. Once I got into the office, I greeted him but he was quiet. He simply showed me to a seat across the table as he made for a drawer and pulled out some papers from it. Then, he handed me a list.

'Read that,' he said.

I read through.

'What names are those?' He asked me.

'I don't know sir.'

'Those have been identified by the school security as cult members…'

I did not quite understand what the man meant.

'Your name is there, meaning you have been identified by the security officers as a cultist!'

'Sir?'

'What happened on the day a student was shot dead in your class? What was your role?'

I sat mute.

'Were you there when the boy was shot dead?'

'Yes, I sat just beside him…' I said feverishly.

'The report here says you are a cultist then. And you were involved in the death of the boy. What this means is that, the university is considering advising you to withdraw from this school since cultists are not harboured in this distinguished institution!'

'No sir, I am not… How could I be a cultist?' My eyes were wet already.

'You are Ondoaka, I suppose?'

'Yes sir, I am Aondoakaa.'

In my state of confusion, I began to tell the man how my mother was going through a lot just to see me through school. How could I join cultism in jeopardy of Mama's effort? The man listened quietly. When I ended, he simply asked me to go back to my hostel. I left the office heavy hearted. How could anyone have listed me as a cultist? Was the HOD making the story up?

I stood by the balcony, feeling dizzy. As I looked across the campus from the balcony, my eyes went to the Students Relaxation Park downstairs. Plants in the park had begun to wither. It was rather too early for plants to begin to wither at the time, but they were withering anyway. It was obvious that my life too had started withering early.

A month passed. Aker and I spent much time together. Tabi called sometimes. I always asked after Mama. The last time she said Mama had gone to Makurdi that week to attend the Zonal Women Christian Fellowship.

Results of our exams were released and pasted on a notice board at the HOD's office. That morning, I went to check my performance. The HOD saw me as he came to his office. I prayed the man would not recognize me, but he did. As he walked towards me, he grinned widely. And then to my surprise, he congratulated me.

'I saw your results, Ondoaka! You are on the very top of the department. I am extremely proud of you!' he said. 'If you continue this way, I bet you will make your mother proud and also have a very great future too!' The man had an accent, but he spoke so slowly that it wasn't hard to get him.

Clearly, the man could see my confusion. Whatever he was saying sounded rather strange to me. Maybe, this is why he asked me to check the scoreboard and see him later that evening in his house at the Senior Staff Quarters. When he entered his office, the full import of the news suddenly hit me. I became so excited that I started to run to the scoreboard, even though I was only a few feet away from it.

I reached the board and began to check the list. Soon, I saw my matriculation number. The names of students were not listed but it was easy to trace one's result with the matriculation number. My result was staring glamorously at me! It wasn't just the best out of the rest; it was a First Class; a GPA of 4.79 out of the 5.0 benchmark! That was a remarkable First-Class result! I had made a first class from my very first semester result in the university!

The excitement in my mind went on even when I returned to the hostel.

The evening was cold when I arrived Professor Ebube's house. It had rained earlier in the afternoon. The professor had just returned from the office. His red Mercedes car was parked outside his house under a tree. I went to the door and knocked. The door was ajar but I waited outside till a voice from the house asked me in. I pushed the door and entered.

Professor Ebube was in the bedroom. He called out that he would be with me in the sitting room soon. The Professor, I was told, had no family. Rumour had it that the man once had an *oyibo* wife who ran away just a year after they returned to the country from the UK. A classmate had once said she ran away because Ebube refused to make love with her while she was cooking in their kitchen.

While I waited in the sitting room, I noticed the floor of the room was stained with mud that the man had brought in, so I went for a mop that was kept beside the kitchen door, took it and began to wipe the floor. Professor Ebube came out from the bedroom when I had just finished mopping the floor and was returning the swab to the kitchen door. 'Thank you, my good friend,' he said as he went to the television and switched it on.

The TV set made a fizzling sound before it came up. The 6 o'clock news was still on. The news item was devastating: A bomb had exploded in a place called Suleja. Cars went up in blazes and children and adults lay roasted like bodies of the Japs who in the martial recklessness of the Hitler War in Hiroshima littered everywhere. A child hawker, barely seven years old, who had been selling oranges in a tray on the streets was shattered by the explosive such that it was absolutely impossible to assemble her strewn limbs into one identifiable figure. It was appalling! That was the first time our country had experienced such an explosion. What used to be heard of in *Oyibo* lands had crept into the country.

Later, a group called Boko Haram would claim responsibility for the attack.

In the days that would follow, the ambience of Kano in the far North would be wrecked by explosives too. The city would be stripped bare; its streets littered with hewed pieces of human flesh and the soil soaked with blood. Odour from the decaying bodies would invite vultures from the sky. People thinking it was all going to end there would have to think again as a town known as Maiduguri would almost be wiped out in series of explosive attacks.

In a while, there appeared a government spokesman on the TV condemning the Suleja attack.

'It's a dastardly act. And the Federal government frowns at it'.

The well shaved and handsome man spoke in a soft voice, prolonging words in an act. 'The government is appealing for calm from citizens. There is no need for panic,' he assured. According to him, it wasn't clear yet if the Suleja bombing was a terrorist attack. 'What is obvious to us now is that an obsolete shell which was not properly disposed of during the Biafra War has unfortunately gone off. The government is right on top of this situation', the spoke man continued.

Prof Ebube hissed and began to rain insults on the spokesman.

While we were completely engrossed in this piece of sad news, there was a knock on the door. A very beautiful young woman came in. She walked across the sitting room towards the professor. A generator at the back of the bathroom was making some sort of kpa-kpa-kpa noise continually and sending some smoke into the room. There was power outage so the professor was using his generator, the kind people called "I pass my neighbour" literally meaning, 'I am better off than my poor neighbours because I am using a small generator.' The situation of power supply on campus had gone so bad that lecturers who used generators could brag that they were able to afford power while others remained in darkness after public supply of electricity was ceased.

'This girl, any time you want something you go come dey shake nyash, abi?' The professor said jokingly to the guest.

'Abegi, Prof, don't you like the nyash?' She went and gave the man a hug. They laughed lightly.

With the girl in the room, my eyes could only roam from wall to wall until they finally stopped at a portrait of the professor that hung above the bedroom door.

When the girl had sat with the man on the sofa, he introduced me to her as the best student in the department.

'He is our only first-class gentleman in the department,' the professor emphasized. The girl greeted me casually, waving her left hand. I had seen the face previously, several times perhaps. The young woman was a classmate. Though we were not course mates, we had a number of lectures together. It was during those lectures that I had seen her. I wanted to return her greeting but did not know what to say, so I sheepishly turned to the TV and continued to stare.

'Ondoaka, Anita is a friend', the professor turned to me and said in a casual voice, as if he did not want to introduce the girl.

'Yes sir,' I said, swallowing a catch that rose in my throat as our eyes met. My eyes returned almost immediately to the wall and continued searching until they settled on the professor's portrait again. Professor Ebube had the shot taken somewhere abroad, the background setting suggested England or so. In his youth, his light complexion could be mistaken for a person of mixed race, what Nigerians call half-cast. The picture must have been taken in the man's late 20s. It appeared Professor Ebube was getting even more handsome with age, particularly, with the way he kept his beards well-trimmed.

'Ondoaka,' the professor called as my eyes moved away from the portrait. 'Things have changed significantly between my generation and yours. And sometimes I wonder if we can ever have back in this country the beauty of the yesteryears. You see, when I was an undergraduate in the University of Nigeria, Nsuka, we would be served tea and eggs for breakfast and chicken for lunch. Your generation does not know what that means, yet the generation does not even know what it has missed!

'In our time, when one graduated, a car was waiting as a gift from the government- this too your generation does not know. I was given a car on my graduation day! You see?' The professor smiled as if he would say 'It's unfortunate that your generation has done so much wrong to deprive itself of the good-old-days.' But instead he said, 'Well, if I have to apportion any blames, I guess I will blame us for not handing over to you all what we benefitted.' I wanted to ask why the government stopped providing chickens for university undergraduates as meals but could not as my eyes shyly went to the TV again.

'Ondoaka, you know why I am proud of you?' he asked. I shook my head quietly. 'You seem to know that it is your responsibility to recover the past we did not hand you and also build a future for yourself which your generation is destroying.' The man cleared his throat as Anita turned and our eyes met briefly.

'Your generation is overwhelmed by terrible things such as cultism- they don't even know what it is. Do they even know how cultism began in Nigerian Universities?' As if expecting an answer from me, the professor stared for a while before he said, 'A man called Wole Soyinka, and his "Magnificent Seven" in 1952 started this whole mess!' The professor edged on his seat. 'Soyinka was a student in the University of Ibadan at a period when *Oyibos* teaching there took pleasure in dehumanizing students, like they did in South Africa. Soyinka said that was wrong. So he started a Pan-Africanist cabal- a cult group, the Pyrates, to disarm the cat which came to steal meat from the child's palm. And I honestly believe Soyinka was doing a beautiful thing. If a man visits your house and sits to wait patiently for food, you should allow him to stay as long as he wants. But if he goes behind your back, ties up your wife's hands and seals her mouth to steal *Nkwobi* from her kitchen and expects no one to talk about it, you must show him the way out of your house, at all cost.' The man coughed before he continued, 'By the way, a man who eats *Nkwobi* and scratches hastily his anus without properly washing hands should not blame the cook for spicing the meat a lot.' I understood that he meant the *Oyibo's* hands had dug too deep into Nigeria and were to expect any outcome.

'When Soyinka left the university, but the cabal continued until it began to spread to other universities. Soyinka became a professor and continued his war on the visitor in his books. And this too was good. But as if the visitor had realized his error and wanted to beg the house owner, he took Soyinka to his land and slammed on him the title of Nobel laureate. Or was that the visitor's way of saying! "*You talk too much about us, shut up?*"

'When Soyinka returned from the visitor's land, his eye turned instead onto the woman who was cooking the *Nkwobi* which the *oyibo* had eyed with watery mouth- he faced the government fiercely.' Professor Ebube's hands gestured now. 'Ondoaka, you know what I would have done if I was Soyinka?'

I shook my head. Anita looked at me from the corner of her eye as if to say, "You Mr. First Class, so you don't have an idea of what you would have done?"

The professor cleared his throat, 'I would have gone round all the universities in Nigeria to kill, in my life time, the plant of cultism I had cultivated. You see?' The professor stared at me for a while, maybe disappointed that I could say nothing. Then he shook his head and turned to the TV.

Uneasily, my eyes joined his at the TV before I turned to the window and realized it was getting dark. I informed the man that I would like to return to the hostel. He coughed, apologized and made for a purse on the glass table in front of him from which he drew a few Naira notes. He handed me the money and added: 'See me tomorrow, Saturday please.' I collected the notes gratefully, thanked him and left.

I kept thinking about everything the professor had said until the name 'Anita' came to mind so strongly that I began to wonder at how beautiful she was.

The next day after I had washed my clothes, I went to see Professor Ebube as he had requested. When I got to the house, I saw that the man's car was not parked outside under the tree which meant that he was not at home. But the *I-pass-my-neighbour* generator was sounding behind the house. Also, the lights in the sitting room were on. So I went to the door and knocked.

'Come in,' a voice answered.

I pushed the door slightly and entered. It was Anita. She was lying on the sofa with an old novel that had a torn cover in her hand. She asked me to lock the door. I did. As I walked across the room, I noticed that her dress stopped half way down her legs exposing the laps slightly as she crossed her legs on the arm of the sofa. We greeted, and I went and sat at the dining table.

'Prof is not in', Anita informed me. 'He has gone to town to watch a football match. He said you should wait in the house until he returns. There is food in the kitchen and orange juice in the fridge. What do you care for?' Even though I was hungry, I told her I was okay. That was how Mama had trained me, to decline food offered by people I did not know very well. When I was a little boy, Mama would even tell me terrible stories of children who accepted food from strangers and met with horrible fortunes.

'There is terrible heat in this room…' the girl broke the silence that had lasted for a while between us. But I kept quiet, not knowing what to say. She said she felt like taking off her shirt. It wasn't a shirt really, just a piece of fabric that ran over her chest, held up by tiny ropes over the shoulders and with buttons running down the front. She unbuttoned the blouse so that I could see the breasts as they stood out like ripe citrus fruits. The sight of her nudity reminded me of Eliza and my throat began to dry up. In as much as I was avoiding the sight, my eyes kept straying there. Suddenly, I began to feel a craving to run my fingers down those breasts like Eliza would run her fingers down my crotch.

I was lost in thoughts of Eliza for a while; the more I thought about Eliza, the more my throat dried up. For once, I wished I had yielded to her wishes. This aroused a keen desire in me to run my fingers down Anita's breasts. The way the girl spread her legs attracted me too. As soon as my eyes went there, I could see her pants underneath her clothes.

Moments passed.

'Prof says you made a First Class?' The girl asked, eventually.

I swallowed before I nodded.

'Were you in Dr. Ayoala's lecture yesterday?'

I nodded again, 'I was.' I said.

She made for the glass table and picked an exercise book on it. 'Can you please come over and put me through something I did not understand during the lecture?'

I nodded and sighed but remained sitting until she beckoned. I got up from the dining table and walked across the room to the sofa to sit where she had made space for me. I swallowed again.

'You seem not to feel the heat in this room. The fan is not helping...'

'I can feel the heat actually,' I said throatily.

'Yet you have these clothes on?'

I stammered and replied that I had adapted to the heat already. My eyes were again running across the wall. What would happen if the professor returned and saw me there, with the girl, in that fashion? I kept asking in my mind.

The girl opened a page in the exercise book and showed me a piece of writing that I could hardly make out. But while I strained my eyes to pick the words, her left hand rested on my lap. A lump rose in my throat. I managed to swallow. But the hand was only going further into my trousers to my crotch and I could not deny knowledge of what was coming. Her fingers now touched my penis. I shivered like I did when Eliza's fingers ran on the organ. My eyes strained on the writing, but the page had become blank and devoid of words. Anita chuckled as her fingers caressed my organ. The chuckle turned to a dry crackle from her throat; and was followed by series of deep breaths. 'You have a huge and lengthy penis,' she sighed.

The woman's nudity was becoming more tormenting.

Up to that point, I had made out no word from the book, only swallowing again and again.

'Anita, please…'

'Make love to me, please,' she begged me.

My heart was thumping hard but the girl would not stop chuckling. As she looked into my eyes, I could feel her succulent lips crush mine. The eagerness throbbed into a quivering heart when I heard the professor's car engine die under the tree outside. It was as if my heart would come out from my mouth.

Anita was hurrying to wear her shirt when a knock came from the door, 'kon-kon', it was followed by the man's impatient voice.

The moment the Professor walked in was an ordeal. He was staring at me steadily as he came, and his face was expressionless. But what was more troubling was the way the man hissed every now and then as he made his way to the sofa.

'I cannot imagine this! Six is unimaginable.' The way he dragged words with an accent made his pronunciation of 'six' sounded as if the 'i' in the middle of the word was replaced with an 'e.' 'It should not have happened!' He continued. This time, his hissing had became deliberately lengthy. 'Arsenal loses a very crucial match by six to zero and to such a small and feeble club side? I can't even explain how that happened! For as much as I am concerned, all the blame is on our good-for-nothing goalkeeper this time. The useless keeper was merely sleeping there in the goalpost!'

The professor sat quietly for a while before he finally turned to me, and asked, 'Ondoka, when did you come?'

'Around 5pm sir'.

'You don't watch football matches. Do you?'

'No sir,' I replied.

He shrugged. 'I can tell', he said, then he rose and walked across the sitting room to his bedroom. Anita who had been sitting on the arm of the chair beside the man stood up and followed him into the room. It was when he was almost at the door to entering the bedroom that he turned and said he would take his bath before joining me. The two disappeared behind the curtains.

Anita came out soon. She sat on the arm of the sofa and crossed her right leg over the left, shaking the suspended foot. Her right hand swept the sofa until it eventually found my phone which she took and dialed her number. As she saved my number in her phone, I heard the shower in the professor's bathroom running.

Anita sat there staring at the TV. In the short time I knew her, she wasn't much of a TV enthusiast. While she stared at the TV, I could nearly hear her speak with me in the mind. At a point she would look at me from the corner of her eye and then smile to herself. This went on for nearly thirty minutes.

The professor did not come to the sitting room again.

I got up and told Anita I was leaving. She tried to persuade me to stay but when she realized I was adamant she said, 'I will call you tomorrow and meet with you in the lecture halls after church'.

On Sundays which were church days, lecture halls were usually quiet as most students returned to the hostels to do their laundry after church.

The next morning, I had just returned to my room from Campus Fellowship when Anita called me on phone. 'I am waiting outside your hostel', her voice came on the phone. I left the room indecisively to see the girl. When I got to the gate of the hostel, I saw Anita waiting in a car, in the driver's seat. I walked over and we greeted. She said she had changed her mind; that instead we would go to her house in town. 'Come into the car let's go', she said.

I walked across, opened the door and took the front seat.

'It's my mum's car,' she said.

'Oh, okay,' I returned.

The feeling as I sat in that car was overwhelming. I had this new sense of importance, even though with an air of inferiority. Sitting there in the car, it was as if the entire world was watching me grow up into a person of worth. Growing up in a little village like Akan where a car was seen only once in years made this moment with Anita a revered one for me. As Anita started the car and we began to drive slowly away, I wished we were driving to Akan.

Back in Akan, if a visitor came to one's house in a car, neighbours talked about it for days.

The car was moving with such elegance that even when Anita said, 'My mum is the Special Adviser to the State Governor on Women Affairs,' I could only nod like the proverbial lizard whom it was said fell from a great height and applauded itself.

'I spoke to my mum about you this morning and she requested that I take you home. She would like to meet you.'

'Meet me?' I asked with a bit of shock. Anita smiled and nodded. The smile had hardly died when her hand rested on my lap. I pushed the hand gently aside. 'You will like my mum when you two meet, she is a simple woman. Sometimes, I say she is the best mum in the world.' Anita said after a while.

'Would she like to meet me?' I asked.

Anita smiled, 'Mum is a very busy woman. She is running for the deputy governor's seat next year, so she has been pressing her buttons. You understand what I mean? But she assured me she would be waiting at home this afternoon for you.'

'Oh,' I returned.

We were already moving toward the school gate at the Main Campus. The air conditioner in the car was on and a soft tune played on the car stereo. We had just passed the school gate when we ran into a police checkpoint that was built on the road with wood-logs and old containers filled with sand. When the logs were lifted, the space allowed just a car through. Two policemen stood behind the roadblock and signalled until we slowed to a halt. It was after the car halted that I saw a soldier who sat on an exposed root of a tree near the road. A rifle lay against the tree beside the man. He was certainly a member of the roadblock team but appeared to be engaged in a sort of private duty.

Since the Suleja bomb explosion, soldiers began to work with the police in what was referred to as the Special Joint Task-Force to improve security, especially on the roads.

'All these rogues again!' Anita hissed.

'Who?' I asked.

'You don't know that these people are thieves in government uniforms?' She asked pointing at the security officers.

'Oh,' I replied.

One of the policemen walked to Anita's window. She wound the glass half way down with a straight face and said, 'Officer.'

The policeman simply replied 'From where to where?'

'School to house.' Anita said.

'Which school?' The policeman continued.

'The university. It's obvious, officer', she answered.

'Big Madam, we dey duty for road,' the man said, searching our eyes.

'Madam, road hard…' he added, grinning. Anita was quiet; her fingers were tapping the steering, straight faced, staring forward.

'Madam, mouth dry. We dey for road. Here na barracks for us these days o!' The policeman smiled sheepishly.

'Soja go soja come, barracks remain. Madam, any cold water for us?' The man seemed to be losing his patience. He removed his dark glasses and peered into the car as if wondering whether the girl had not been hearing him. Anita was still quiet.

'Madam, road hard! Abi you no dey hear?'

The girl smiled and shook her head. 'Officer, allow us to go, please,' she said.

That was enough to upset the police officer completely. The man cocked his gun, his face totally devoid of any trace of friendliness.

'Come outside! Ashawo! You are a suspect! Bring your particulars! Abi you think sey na play we come play for here? We mean business! Come down! Quick, quick!' He began to fume.

Anita was now smiling but her face hardened with arrogance when the man made for the door and pulled it open. I had never seen a face more fierce than the policeman's.

'Come down! Your father! Criminal! Abi na play you think we come play for here? We de enter station straight, suspect!'

The soldier under the tree lifted his head and looked at us briefly and then returned to his engagement.

Anita refused to step out of the car, her hand still held on to the steering. The man cocked the gun again. 'We dey go station! You hear me?' He fumed.

'And you will lose your job there when my mother comes!'

This angered the man even more. 'Your mother na Queen Elizabeth of England? Come down jare, idiot!' The voice cracked with fury.

'She is not Queen Elizabeth but the governor's special adviser. And that is enough to take your miserable work from you today when she comes!'

The policeman shrugged and then relented, 'Na your mama be governor adviser?' The voice was resuming its normalcy. 'You for tell me since.' The man had withdrawn from the door almost completely now.

'Yes, my mother is the governor's special adviser, if you care to know, Officer.'

The man lowered his rifle and lowered his voice even more. 'Madam, sorry, but you for tell me before. Your mama na better woman,' he said.

'Can we go then?' Anita smiled victoriously to herself.

'Sure Madam!' The man saluted and shut the door. 'Carry go Madam,' he said.

Anita did not thank the man but instead hissed as we began to drive away. I wondered the kind of fabric most police officers were made of in our country. It was becoming increasingly easy for most policemen to soil the soul of their integrity. Anita was driving slowly now. We were approaching town. *Okadas* or commercial motorcycles were all over the place. Motorcycle riding had assumed appreciable dimensions not just in Urokpa-West but also in Makurdi. Someone had once written in the papers how the business had become a thirst-quencher for youths who were bedevilled by unemployment. Even graduates were fast basking in the euphoria of the industry. But the situation was not as bad as one who read that paper column might conclude. Perhaps, the reader would have developed the ability to see things from the eye of a writer's pen.

Anita negotiated a right turn at the roundabout where a traffic warden was controlling traffic. Those *Yellow fevers* were something else! Their acrobatic display as they halted and let traffic through never failed to fascinate me. It was more or less like the acrobatic dance of the 'Snake

Girl' performed by little girls in Côte d'Ivoire in which the supple young girls writhed and coiled as though they were snakes and were then tossed into the air by men who appeared to catch them on the tips of knife blades. The acrobatics appeared to be a fine way to show publicly how much one could love one's duty. Motorists sometimes recognized that love for duty when they squeezed a note and threw it at the *yellow fevers*.

The traffic officers had earned the name, *yellow fever,* from the bright orange colour of their uniforms which people considered as yellow. Why not? The colour of their shirts bore semblance to the hue of the eyeballs of those infected with the jaundice also know as Yellow Fever.

We drove a little into a street then Anita pulled to a stop at a green gate. The gatekeeper, a tubular old man, came, peeped through a hole in the gate and opened the gate. We drove in.

The house was magnificent but I had little time to look around as Anita and I came out from the car and walked to the door of the building. She pressed a knob which opened the door. She let me walk in before she followed and shut the door.

A television set was on in the sitting room which was 3 or 4 times the size of Professor Ebube's. Seats were arranged in a crescent around the TV. There was also a freezer, some artificial flowers and few other items. Anita showed me to a seat, turned and disappeared into one of the rooms. In a moment, she returned and informed me that her mum would be with me shortly. She turned and disappeared again.

After some minutes, a door opened and Joseph Eugene, my classmate, walked in. He was called 'Capo' by his friends in school. It was whispered among our classmates that the boy was a cultist, and Capo was his rank name in the cult. Several times, Joseph had left during classes, gone and smoked, then returned while a lecture went on. At other times, he and his friends sat in the Coca-cola Park and ignored lectures.

I hailed him by his name, Joseph. He looked briefly at me, gave no response, turned and disappeared into one of the rooms. He almost collided with Anita who was bringing a glass of fruit juice for me.

'You know my brother, don't you?'

'You mean Joseph?'

'Yeah, Joe.'

'I do. We are classmates. Others call him Capo?'

'He doesn't answer that name here in the house. Mum will not allow him.'

Later, I would learn that Joe and Anita were Igbos like Jaja and Kambili whose stories were told in *Purple Hibiscus*.

'But I had no idea that you two are related.'

'Oh, we are.'

Anita had barely completed the sentence when her mother walked into the sitting room. Except for the mother's plumpness, they were exact copies. I stood and greeted her, bowing. The woman urged me to sit but I waited for her to take a seat before I sat myself. Anita sat on the arm of her mother's chair. She leaned closer and whispered into her mother's ear. Her mother smiled as she looked at me, and then I heard the words spoken softly, 'Handsome, tall, and humble too.' Anita smiled too. I was staring at the floor.

'My son, welcome,' Anita's mother said.

'Thank you Ma,' I replied. She turned to her daughter and asked if I had eaten. Anita said the house maid was preparing something for me.

'My son, Anita says you and Joseph are in the same class?'

'Yes Ma,' I replied.

'You know he is my son?'

'Anita just told me a while ago, Ma.' I said.

She turned and gave her daughter a why-did-you-not-tell-him-earlier look. She returned to me and beckoned, 'Come and sit here beside me.'

I went and sat on the chair beside her while Anita went to check if my food was ready.

'My son, you know Joe, you said?'

'Yes Ma. We are classmates.' I answered.

'That boy wants to embarrass me,' the woman sighed.

'I have two boys. His elder brother is doing very well, studying medicine in America. As for Joe, I have done everything I can. This is his third admission into the university. He doesn't even complete his first year before they send him away. And then, I have to go looking for another school. When Joe was a child, I sent him to the best schools. What have I done wrong that I now deserve constant embarrassment from him?'

'I am sorry Ma,' I said.

'My son, is that how to pay back a mother who loves a child?'

I was quiet as I did not know what to say.

'Is this how you treat your mother, my son?'

I shook my head from side to side; 'No Ma'.

'Why don't you treat your mother badly?' Her eyes searched mine for a while but when I offered no response, she sighed.

'Well, when Anita told me of you, I said she should plead with you to come see me. Maybe you can help me with this boy.'

Anita had just come from the kitchen with some pieces of fried yam in a plate and kept it on a side table beside me. My eyes went to the yams briefly. The woman asked Anita where her brother was. 'He is in his room,' she replied and went to call him.

'I am thinking you can really help me with this boy,' the woman said. Her hand made for mine but stopped half way on the chair.

'Ma, I will do anything possible to help,' I said.

'Anything possible?' she edged on her seat and asked again, 'You will do anything possible, you say?'

I smiled in response.

The ceiling fan spun overhead steadily.

'Money is not a problem,' she said and then asked again if I could do anything possible to help.

'I won't help for money. I feel obliged to be of help, if I can, in any way. Not for money at all.' I said.

The woman was searching my eyes when Anita returned from Joseph's room. In a while, Joseph came in too.

Anita took her position on the arm of the chair beside her mother while Joe sat far off from us. 'Joseph, do you know this young man?' His mother asked him.

'I do,' he answered throatily. His mother spoke to him for long, telling him how I was doing well in school. After she was done, the boy stood up quietly and left for his room again. The woman turned to me and asked, 'Have you seen that attitude?'

'I am sorry Ma', I answered.

'That is how Joe is paying me for taking good care of him.'

The woman stared into the air steadily and then, as if something had sprung into her mind, she beckoned on me to draw closer.

'You see, my son, I want you to help me. I want you to help me with this boy.'

I was listening.

'Do you know that during the last exams, Joe passed only three papers? And he did not even pass those three with good grades!'

'Oh,' I said.

'I am telling you my son. And now, I am afraid that they will soon send him out of school again if something is not done quickly.'

The woman drew even closer and whispered, 'Please, will you allow Joe to copy from you during exams? I understand that that kind of thing can be arranged for. Or would you prefer to be writing his papers after you complete yours?'

A lump rose in my throat and I swallowed.

'You see, you don't have to be scared. I know your Vice Chancellor very well. I know him very well. And if it is money you want, money is no problem. I am sure you are following me?'

I understood what the woman meant but I had suddenly lost my voice. She laughed desperately. 'My son, I am sure you are following the plan?'

'Yes, Ma,' I said.

In a moment of silence, Mama's words never to do what my mind doubts streamed into my head pricking my conscience. But then, there was some good, certainly, in being of some sort of assistance to a woman in dire need.

'Yes Ma, I understand what you mean.' I nodded.

'Good! Good, my son, good.' The woman's face brightened up as her hand finally touched mine, rubbing slowly.

'Good, my son, good,' she kept repeating

In the following days, things became rosy between Anita and I.

She would come and fetch me from the hostels in the evenings for studies in the lecture rooms just as she did that evening when we were waiting by the Students Union Park for Aker. Aker had forgotten a book in his room and had gone to get it. While waiting there at the park, we saw Joe come by the walkway from the Coca-cola Park with a friend of his. Joe had a kind of dancing gait, especially when he was walking slowly. Anita mentioned that she had not seen him since that day when I was in their house. I told her I too had not seen the boy for that long. She wondered where he had disappeared to. We laughed when I said maybe he had gone to the moon.

Joe and his friend got to us and he shook hands with me. 'Ondoaka, I can see you are getting on very well with my sister,' he said. But I only smiled in return. He shrugged, said it was okay and then turned to his sister and told her to take good care of me. I felt it was kind of him to say such a thing.

Later that evening, when we were reading in a lecture room, Joe came again and called his sister out. They talked for a while before Anita returned. She told me her brother wanted to talk to me too. Aker was sitting beside me while Anita sat across the desk. I left them and joined Joe outside the classroom.

'Joe,' I greeted.

The boy cleared his throat, 'My name is not Joe but Capo.' I corrected myself and called him Capo. Even then, he only cleared his throat and said something very strange. He said that a rumor was going around the university campus that I was a cultist and he wanted to hear from me if I was one. I was shocked to hear this. But it wasn't entirely strange to me as earlier, my name had appeared on Professor Ebube's list as a cultist.

Joe looked at me with a stone face and told me he was a cultist. I squinted but he insisted that he meant it. He said I was in a very bad position at the moment, and he wanted me to understand that. I replied that I was not a cultist and had no Intention of becoming one; if anyone had such a terrible misconception about me, it was very unfortunate. But Joe informed me that a rival cult group was already planning to attack me as a result of the circulating rumour. I could read the seriousness of the claim in his eyes.

'My God, why is this happening to me?' I sighed.

'It is not the best time to ask God stupid questions. Danger is coming. And you must take active steps as a man', he advised. Even in the lecture hall where I was sitting with Anita and Aker, he said he had spotted two members of that group who had left when they saw him come to talk to me. I remembered that I had seen two boys leave the hall a while ago.

'I am going to help you, if I you are willing to help yourself''.

'I see', I said.

'My sister cares about you. This is why I am concerned. I am doing this for her. All I am doing is to protect her happiness'.

The boy's hand made for his pocket and he brought out a carefully folded piece of paper.

'It's a confidential form. Complete it and return it to me tomorrow before you go for lectures.' He emphasized again that the piece of paper was confidential and reminded me to be careful on campus. 'Don't let the paper get missing', he cautioned. I collected the paper, thanked him and returned to join Anita and Aker.

That night, when I returned to the hostel, I completed the form. On the top left was written, "CAN Approved". As far as I knew, CAN meant Christian Association of Nigeria. It meant nothing special to me at that time but later I would realize that CAN also meant Confraternity Association of Nigeria. This was not a Christian Association of Nigeria form. It was a rite for brotherhood of a cult. I blindly wrote my name, age, sex, home address in the village and a few other things like agreeing to terms and conditions and then I appended my signature and wrote the date.

The next morning after I had my bath and was leaving for class, I went to Capo's room and gave him the completed form. He said we needed to see in the evening, by 8p.m. 8p.m was quite late for me to see anyone but he insisted it was very important for us to see that evening so I assured him that I would see him. Coca-cola Park was where I was to meet him.

I had no lectures that day. A senior lecturer in Physics Department had died, and in his honour, all lectures were cancelled. I returned to the hostel and Aker and I spent the day together.

In the evening, birds flying in the sky could be seen silhouetted against the crimson orb of the sinking sun. When twilight approached, I headed for the Coca-cola Park. The bar had closed. Students had deserted the place except for two young men who sat in a corner. When I got into the bar, I realized one of them was Capo.

'Capo', I greeted and we shook hands before I took a seat. Capo led a discussion of recent happenings on campus as we sat listening. In a while, we were joined by three other young men.

An hour later, the SU president and one other young man joined us. This was around 7:49p.m. Soon, the chap who came with the SU president pulled out a pistol from under his trousers and kept it on the table. He was unloading it. It was only then that I finally realized where I was and what I was getting myself into; I had inadvertently completed the first phase of the initiation process into cultism which was signing of the CAN agreement form.

The second stage of my initiation had begun, something called "Blending." It would involve physical torment, a test of my courage and endurance. By physical torture, my endurance would be tested after which I would blend in with the confraternity, Joe had said plainly. I sat quietly, listening.

This evening too, electric power had failed. Like other days when there was no light, students went back to the hostels early. Dogs went round scavenging for food. We could hear them fighting somewhere not too far from the park.

I wished I could vanish into thin air. I began to think of the possibility of escaping but remembered a story about a student who was killed by cultists when he attempted to run away during an initiation process. His body was riddled with bullets and machete wounds. The horrible memory of the murdered student became even more vivid in my mind. I was shivering. If it were daylight, Capo would have noticed me shivering. I thought of telling Capo that I had forgotten food that I was cooking on the stove in the hostel and I wanted to go put out the light. Of course it was a lie, but it was an escape plan. But what if he called someone on the phone in the hostel and asked the person to go off the stove for me? I thought of getting up and running like a scared rat, but they would chase me or simply shoot me down, and no one would ever know the exact story. I became terrified.

Capo and his gang were waiting for one more new convert from another university to join us. I sat there, still thinking of the best way to escape. Then I turned to Capo confidently and thanked him for the opportunity granted me to have their "imperative" security.

'I am truly grateful and excited about this unique opportunity to be a part of this fraternity', I said.

He was happy to hear that. When he returned to his discussion again, I interrupted, 'I am pressed my brother. I want to ease myself around the corner'.

'Okay, be fast about it. We will soon start', he said.

I stood up, unzipping my trousers as if I was going to pee there right away, then hurried towards the direction of the fighting dogs at the back of the park. Behind the park was a bush path that led to the school waterboard. I followed it, tiptoeing as fast as I could. I felt someone following me. It was a terrifying moment. To make it difficult for anyone following me, I turned into the bush and began to run in the dark. I missed my way to the hostel.

I had run very far into the bush before I stopped. It was dark everywhere. I sat on the ground in the bush, suppressing my panting as much as I could. In the quietness of the night, I would have heard footsteps now if anyone was following me. Apparently, they did not suspect I wanted to escape so no one had attempted to follow me. Mosquitoes began to buzz around my ears.

It was hours before light was restored. I could now see my hostel in the distance, almost a kilometer or two away. If not for the mosquitoes, I would have stayed there till dawn.

I took off my shirt to avoid being seen and began to trace my way back to the hostels. This was around 2 or 3 am. Finally, when I got back to the hostel, I went to Aker's room and slept there.

The next morning, we had a lecture. During the lecture, Capo was absent. Instead, Sala who usually sat with Edau by the door had taken Capo's accustomed seat. After the lecture, as I was hurrying out I saw Capo standing against a pole in front of our lecture hall with a cigarette between his lips, staring into space.

'Capo', I greeted him. The stony face loosened in a brief smile then, he began to shake his head in a way that was clear he was pitying me.

As I walked pass, he said, 'I pity you, Ondoakaa'.

I stopped and allowed the words to sink in before I shook my head and walked away.

In the evening, we were in the lecture hall again, Anita, Aker and I. This evening, only a few students had come to read as most students had gone to town for the weekend. There was power failure again and we were using candlelight to read.

Anita said she wanted to go and ease herself and wanted me to escort her. Aker made a joke of it that at her age, she was still scared of the dark. We all laughed lightly and then Anita and I left while Aker still sat there reading.

At Anita's prompting, we headed for the Physics Relaxation Park several blocks away from the lecture halls. I knew she wanted to have me to herself in a lonely place. Like the lecture halls, the park too was deserted and dark.

Once we settled in a metallic seat, Anita started running her hands all over me. One hand sank into my trousers, made for my crotch and began to caress my already aroused penis. A picture of Eliza flashed in my mind and I unabashedly slipped my hand under Anita's skirt, letting my fingers hunt for the wetness of the bald mound between her legs. While our hands explored and administered pleasure, our lips drank of the heady sweetness of our mouths. Eventually, we made love there in the park. I cannot tell ashamed I felt after the act.

As we returned to the hall to meet Aker, I was sober, unlike Anita who had become excited, laughing and hanging her hand over me my shoulders. We got to the hall and saw that the candle was still burning there and our books were still on the reading table where we had left them but Aker was not there. We saw him lying on the floor at the foot of the table in a pool of blood, grunting in pain. Hurriedly, I sat him up.

Between groans, Aker said, 'Two students came asking after you. I told them you were not around but one of them insisted he saw you with me just a while ago here. He got angry and stabbed me with a knife, saying I am hiding you'.

I was dumbstruck.

Aker was bleeding. With the use of one of the commercial motorcycle on campus, we helped him to the university clinic which was about a kilometer from the spot. When we got to the clinic, there was only a nurse on duty. Even though a security report was needed for his treatment, the nurse mercifully administered First Aid. We supported Aker back to his hostel room. The next morning we would return to see a doctor.

The morning of the next day brought shocking news. Professor Ebube was found dead in his room. The man hung lifeless from a rope tied to the ceiling fan in his sitting room. I knew Professor Ebube very well. A lover of good life, he was not the kind of man who would commit suicide. I was deeply bothered. Even Anita was clearly moved. This was despite her not seeing much of the professor since we became close. When she came to meet me so we could take Aker to the clinic, her eyes were filled with tears. She looked exhausted and worn out.

At the school clinic, it was past 10am but the doctor had not arrived yet.

'He has gone for a meeting', a nurse told us as we sat waiting.

Doctors were planning to embark on an industrial strike action because their salaries were not paid for over four months, it was rumored.

The doctor eventually came in around 11:24am. He went straight to examine Aker. He said that the situation was beyond the services that the university clinic could offer. Aker was bleeding internally. It was a serious situation.

That afternoon, Anita and I made arrangements and sent Aker home to Makurdi through public transport to go and meet his elder sister. I was sure he would get better care there. Daily, I spoke with Tabi on the phone and followed the progress of Aker's health. He was said to be recovering steadily.

Dr. Ayaola had completed a lecture with us barely twenty minutes ago. Being a Friday, our lectures ended by 12:30p.m to give Muslims time for Friday prayers. Already, one could hear the *Allahuakbar* chant from the campus mosque rend the air, mingling with the voices of some of my classmates who were still in the lecture hall.

Thoughts of Mama crossed my mind and I began to reflect on her courage which kept her pushing on in life. Was I still doing everything I could to impress her unflinching commitment to my schooling? Guilt began to envelop me, and the need to write a book in her honour became urgent. Maybe, I would title the book *The Dance of a Golden Mother*. Maybe, it would be *God Slept Upon Her Beauty* or I would simply title the book, *My Mother's Struggles*!

While I was still figuring a suitable title for my mental book, my cell phone began to ring in my left breast pocket, jolting me out of my reverie. I reached for the phone but the ringing stopped. Instead of bringing out the phone to see who it was that had called, I turned and was looking at Ojama, a classmate who sat beside me with Patrick. The duo had been arguing about an English Premiership League match that was played a night ago. In the heat of their argument, Ojama's mouth became an object of ridicule. Patrick pointed out that the mouth had a sagging banana-fruit-shape and laughed mechanically, creating a quick moment of humor for me. I smiled. It was the first time I consciously took note of Ojama's mouth despite our being course mates for close to a year. We were still in our first year in the university.

My phone was ringing again. I looked at its screen and saw that it was Tabi who was calling. With both excitement and worry, I answered with a deep accent that was clearly forced, 'H – a – l – l – o – o – o!' I said. For no particular reason, I remember, a wide smile swept across my face.

'Tabi, *u pande nan*?' I asked in Tiv, enquiring how she was.

But instead of replying with her regular playfulness, she called my name, 'Aondoakaa…'

Before I could mutter a word, she continued, 'Aondoakaa, your friend Aker is dead—'.

'Hello?'

'Aker died…this morning.' Sobs accompanied her words.

'No, this cannot be true…'

I shifted in my seat as a chill ran down my spine. With my eyes wide open, everywhere became dark.

Tabi said softly, 'His corpse has already been moved to Akan and deposited at the mortuary in the new medical center.'

'Tabi, are you joking?' I asked but only to a dead line as Tabi was gone.

'Hello! H–e–llo–o!! Tabi…'

Tabi was as close to Aker as I was. When we were children in the primary school in Akan, Aker had once called Tabi his wife, and Tabi fought him over it. Though Aker had only called her his wife playfully, I had secretly nursed the hope that someday this joke would become reality. Tabi may have had different thoughts but she and Aker had kept that closeness that distance struggles to separate. When Aker was taken to the Federal Medical Center in Makurdi, Tabi went to stay beside his sickbed for days. I had told her over the phone the previous night that she would make a good wife to Aker someday but she had laughed and said it was just her natural way of being supportive and she was there just to feed me with Aker's progress.

I knew Tabi was not joking about Aker's death, she would not joke with something so serious. Tears began to gather in my eyes, blurring my vision as my heart pounded furiously, making the sort of sound boiled yams make in a wooden mortar when a pestle is lifted into the air and returned energetically to crush the yams into smooth edible paste.

'Kpash!' I burst out and flung the phone in annoyance across the lecture room. It cut through the warm afternoon air smoothly and struck the chalkboard on the wall. The phone shattered into pieces on the floor.

Ojama looked briefly at me with his sagging lips parting in

surprise.

I sniffed, then hissed.

I had caused the death of the boy, I thought sadly as I plunged the little finger on my left hand into my nostril, scrubbed roughly and picked a lump of wet mucus on the tip of the fingernail. I shook it off and wiped the finger with the ear of my shirt. A tear drop rolled lazily from my left eye and fell on my shirt. It sank into the fabric. Another tear drop followed. I lay my head on the desk and began to sob helplessly like a child.

When I lifted my head, I looked through the lecture hall's windows to the Relaxation Park where Anita, Aker and I usually relaxed. The park had suddenly lost its allure to me. This was the same park that had once blossomed with beauty, a place I once loved. But, it was not just the park that had lost its beauty to me, the whole university had. In fact, the whole country had suddenly lost its beauty in my mind. Why not? The Nigeria we were growing up in was thinning in its splendor with too many things falling apart. Lack of adequate security in universities was one of them. Lack of youth mentorship was another. How could a generation expected to be the future leaders of a nation be so left alone in its struggles to find its feet? For me, providing a onetime orientation to university students and expecting them to have a well shaped character was inadequate.

In our universities, we spend five days in a week teaching the young letters but hardly do we create seminars or workshops that will improve the character of these young people. Why then do our institutions award degrees in "learning and character" without nurturing the virtues that lead to character improvement? In a generation characterized by information explosion, why do you allow young people to struggle on their own to figure out what is right? Would you sincerely say you are building a generation of future leaders by teaching them letters from books that were written by foreigners before Nigeria gained independence in 1960?

I was fed up with school instantly.

Outside the lecture hall, the sun was shining vivaciously as if proudly saying, 'I like burning hell over this unfortunate place called Africa!' The heat in the lecture hall too had become intense. I dabbed the sweat on my face with the edge of my shirt. Ojama had picked my phone and brought it to me. I noticed how he had Aker's looks: The same pale and sunken eyes, and his nose had the same graceful slimness of a Namibian goat. Several words may have stood behind Ojama's lips, but he stared at me quietly, turned and walked away.

Tired of sitting there with wet eyes, I gathered my books, stood up and began to walk to the door. Somewhere near the chair in front of the lecture room, breeze was dragging a piece of paper on the floor in listless labour. Dr. Ayoola had lobbed the paper there during the lecture. I wiped my face with the back of my hand again. Edau and Sala were staring at me as I walked out. I knew they were waiting for me to leave the room before they started their usual gossips. Even as I walked through the door, I heard their voices. It was Sala's voice that I first heard, 'He is such a pitiable thing!'

There was nothing left for me in that school. All I wanted from that moment was to drop out of the university. I wanted to run away. There was nothing else to do but run.

## Reaping Guinea-corn

### St. Winifred, Akan

I ran back home to Akan.

Walking through the street that led to the church, I saw women breaking firewood in their compounds. The street itself, although almost only a thin and dusty bush-path, was particularly unique. It was the prime identity of a fast-developing Akan. It ran from the market-square through the Health Care Center to St. Winifred Catholic Church; thus, it ran almost through the entire village settlement. Firewood vendors, particularly young mothers, laboured by the street day-after-day to earn their living. The firewood market was growing fast. A surging population of settlers lined the street with firewood for sale.

I saw a friend of Mama's. She too vended firewood by the street. At the moment, she was breaking firewood with an axe. I raised my voice and greeted her from the distance. Even though the axe made much noise on impact with the wood, the woman heard my voice. She stood with the axe still in her hand and stared blankly at me as the harsh rays of the sun blinded her for a while. She grinned and shielded her eyes with one hand, and then recognized me. 'Uwu, Aondoakaa is that you?' she asked joyfully. Her face kept its brilliance for a while before she adjusted her wrapper firmly over her breasts she said, 'welcome', and returned to her labour. Soon, her little daughter came walking to her with faltering steps. The child was naked and catarrh ran down from her nose hanging in a dappled gel across her mouth. The little girl was crying as she walked to the mother. I passed the compound to some ragamuffins playing on a garbage heap under a pawpaw tree.

I waved at the playing children but they were so engrossed none returned my salute. I passed them, negotiated the narrow path that led to our compound in the church. On entering our compound, I saw Eliza walking towards the cashew tree with a clay pot in her hand. She looked up and saw me.

'Aondoa-k-a-a! Aondoa-k-a-a!! Aondoa-k-a-a!!!' The woman dropped the pot on the ground and began to shout with excitement as she ran towards me, her arms stretching out like a bird sailing the skies. Eliza got to me and threw her full weight at me. She leered and took my bag. 'Welcome Mr. University!' she said. I smiled.

When we got to the cashew tree, I saw Mama too as she came out from her hut. She threw away a piece of rag in her left hand and made for me just like Eliza had done. I could not help but call out joyfully, 'Mama!'

'My son!' Mama replied gleefully.

When she got to us, I enquired 'How is the pain in your breast, Mama?'

'It has not completely healed yet but I thank God I am alive', she said before adding 'I didn't know you were coming so soon…' She coughed laboriously. 'Hope you had a nice journey?' she asked.

'Yes, Mama. I thank God'.

We approached her hut. At the door, Eliza handed back my bag, punched me lightly on the shoulder and said, 'You will eat plenty food today!' We all smiled to her utterance as the woman turned and went her way.

'Mama, the journey was well. I have come to see how Aker will be buried next week.'

'Oh, we received the news of the boy's death with great sorrow,' Mama shook her head. 'You have done well by coming,' she said, coughed again and then pushed open the door and we entered the hut.

The room had not changed, except for the water pot that Mama had moved from the door a little inside.

'I know you are hungry…' she said.

'You are very right Mama,' I replied, laughing.

'You won't change!' Mama laughed too. 'Sometimes I wonder if what they are teaching you at the university is how to eat your mother's food! But if that is what they are teaching you, you have a mother, who is a good cook and you don't have to worry.'

'M-a-m-a! They are not teaching me how to like food. But you are right, my mother is a wonderful cook and I can't just stop desiring more of her food.'

Mama laughed again, 'Let me get food for you then...' she said and turned to leave the room but stopped at the door, and asked, 'How is that Professor friend of yours doing?'

'Oh, Professor Ebube? He has been transferred... to another university.' I stuttered, not wanting to break the sad news of the late Professor to Mama under the present circumstance. Mama said it was bad news for her that Ebube was no longer in the school. She had wanted to visit the man with yams someday in appreciation of his kindness and support to me. Her eyes searched mine for a while before she sighed and left the room.

I left the room too, to see Father Gregory. When I came out from the hut, I saw Adu. The child stood by the door of their hut with a bottle of palm-oil in his hands. He did not see me until I got to the priest's house. That was when his little voice came, 'Uncle! Uncle!!' I waved at him. But my eyes went beyond him and caught something that troubled my mind for a while. His father's grave was a mound of soil where a few grasses had begun to grow at the back of the hut. It wasn't only Eliza's husband's grave that was there. Vincent, a seminarian who died several years ago, even before I was born, was buried there too. For a while, I wondered why Father Gregory had insisted that Eliza's husband be buried in the church instead of his village, as was customary in Mbaikyo.

I looked at the graves again. Erosion was washing the mounds away but the grass growing on the graves were more greenish than elsewhere, they were quite distinctive. A little distance away from the churchmen's graves, goats could be seen grazing.

Life was becoming a graveyard I thought. I shook my head, at the same time pushing Father Gregory's parlour door. It was locked. Turning around, I saw Eliza come out of her kitchen and walk across the compound to Adu who was still holding the bottle of palm-oil by the door of the hut.

It was Thursday morning. We were on our way to farm when I informed Mama, I would be going back to school in a week's time. Actually, I hoped to raise some money from her so as to go to a safe haven where I would start a business. If the business prospered, then I would return to Akan and take Mama with me. I hoped that life would be better for her that way. Although, I felt guilty of the deception, it offered the only hope for the happiness I had always desired for her.

Mama breathed heavily and said things were rough for her at the time.

'We have to uproot the groundnuts on the farm to sell by the next market day,' she said. Her words dragged heavily, just like her breath.

I deeply resented lying to Mama. And the agony with which the money had to be raised also worried me. I took a deep breath as she continued, 'sale of the groundnuts is all we can do to raise money at this moment; you know how difficult things are with us at present.'

'Mama, I appreciate all you are doing for me. There can never be a better time for me to assure you that I will not thwart these efforts!'

Mama coughed, 'We will have to work harder during the week to get the nuts ready before the next market day,' she said.

'Fresh groundnuts don't sell at a good price these days, we must get them dried' she added after coughing again.

'Mama, you cough very often lately,' I observed.

'It's the weather.' she replied and coughed again.

After a pause, I said, 'I am aware that fresh groundnuts sell at a ridiculously low price during this period'. Then I sincerely apologized for the stress I was causing her. But of course, Mama was always glad to do even much more for me.

'But how much money do you say you need, my son?' she asked after a while.

'As much money as we are capable of getting...'

Mama went ahead of me with a wicker basket carefully balanced on her head as we walked. A small hoe sat in the basket while I held a machete and followed her closely behind. It had rained during the night and the bush path was still wet with dew. There were puddles of water here and there.

Generally, we went in silence for a while before Mama or I would bring up an issue and we conversed over it briefly. At one time, she said what appeared to be funny but robbed my mind of peace for some time. She was considering that I could start looking for a wife so that after school I could get married. 'Settle down' was the way she put it. We laughed over the issue but I understood what she meant and knew that it wasn't a light matter she had raised. Mama never joked with such issues, except when they weighed too heavily on her mind.

'If the mouth of an old woman refuses to respect strong bones, it will soon learn how to swallow flesh! Eliza says all the time that you are full-grown and I am beginning to see reason with her,' Mama said and laughed, a laugh that lost its weight earlier than its expression.

Her mind must have been occupied with a lot after raising the issue of marriage as we walked the rest of the way to the farm in silence. The sun began to rise when we got to the farm. Passers-by had begun to eat the groundnuts at the edge of the farm close to the road. Two ridges were already rid of groundnut. There was need to uproot the groundnuts before more went into long throats. That Thursday, we had to work even harder so that we could cover the next day's work, because Aker was to be buried in next two days. And I had to go assist his family in preparing for his burial.

We prayed, thanking God for the day and asking for his divine protection, before we began to work.

We harvested the groundnuts in silence.

Mama hardly spoke while working. When it was noon, the sun burnt into our skins intensively. Mama was sweating profusely from the heat of the scorching sun, yet she continued to work as if the groundnuts were coming out easier from the ground by noon.

Mama continued to cough. I pleaded with her that we abort the work for the day. She was adamant but I kept insisting until she conceded to going home.

I went around the farm and collected firewood from dead plants, trimmed them with the machete and then gathered them into the basket. When I was done, Mama took the basket of firewood and headed home while I went the other way through my late friend's house to see how the preparations for his burial was going. Mama had suggested, I follow her home. I would bathe before I returned to visit my late friend's house. But considering the distance, I pleaded with her and went away. As soon as Mama went out of sight, Adu came running to me, driving a bicycle wheel with a dry stick and holding his dirt-stained pant with his left hand to stop it from falling off his waist. The boy got to me and stopped. He was panting heavily like a dog which had run for miles, chasing game.

'What is it Adu?' I enquired.

'Uncle… Uncle…' The boy struggled to catch his breath.

'Uncle, some, some, some men are, are, looking for you at home. They say they want to see you without delay. They have a car, a big car.'

'They want to see me?'

The child nodded.

'They have a car?'

He nodded, 'A big car,' he emphasized again.

'Do you know the men?'

He shook his head.

'How many are they?'

'Two…,' he pointed three fingers at me.

'Is your mother at home?'

He nodded.

I told him, he could go on home. He picked up the bicycle wheel and threw it on a roll, he ensured continuity of the roll with a dry stick and started running home.

'Tell Mama to drop the firewood, I will come and carry it home.' But the lad did not hear a word. Soon, he was out of sight. I followed hastily.

When I approached our compound, Adu sat under the cashew tree playing; building dust in small rectangular mounds. The boy craftily placed a twig across another and tied them together into a cross. He planted it on a mound so that it look similar to the cross on his late father's grave. I looked up and saw a Mercedes car parked away from the cashew tree. Someone was in the driver's seat, another stood at the back of the car. I noticed that, all three men wore black clothes just as the car they had, was also black. The man who stood at the back of the car was speaking to Mama. My concern was that Mama was still carrying the basket with the stack of wood and the hoe on her head. I wondered who the visitor was that could not allow her to bring the basket down before interrogating her with questions. That was when I stopped and took a closer look. I could see that there was also another person in the back seat of the car.

As I worried about the visitors' lack of manners, he suddenly slapped Mama. I heard the sound even behind the cashew tree were I was. My mouth went wide open in shock. I wanted to yell at him to stop but words did not come out of my mouth. At the same time, I looked around quickly to see if anyone else around had seen what had happened. It was only Adu who was playing with sand in front of his mother's hut. The lad lifted his eyes to the noise, searched briefly and went back to his play again.

Mama staggered; the basket lost balance but she quickly supported it with her left hand. At the same time, she started off, running in my direction. The man quickly seized her by the hand and drew her to himself. The basket fell off. The man drew a knife from his belt quickly and in no time Mama darted to the ground with knife stabs. Blood spluttered as she fell to the ground and started jerking.

Everything seemed so unreal. But there was Mama squirming

on the ground, struggling with her last breath. She writhed for a while and then lay still.

I roared, leapt and rushed with the machete at the man who had cut down my mother. In the fury of the moment, I lost sanity and was not conscious of my action. I roared and ran for the man, like a barmy dog. He pulled a pistol and fired at me.

The bullet caught me and knocked the machete off. I fell to the ground on my back, coiled up and was rolling here and there in pains.

I heard footsteps approach. When I looked, I first saw Mama's corpse on the ground not too far away from where I was. And then, I saw Capo! He was the person who had sat in the car. The man who had stabbed mother was still pointing the pistol at me.

'Capo, I want to waste the fool,' the man with the pistol said.

Capo was silent and in the midst of this nightmare, I wondered how the cultists had located me in my village which was several cities away from Urokpa-West. Then I remembered: I had written my home address boldly on the CAN form which I earlier completed and returned to Capo.

'Ondokaa, you are just an idiot,' was the first thing Capo said. His voice was low, as it had always been.

'You are an idiot! You see, you have forced me to squeeze out your pile of shit.' He was smiling and shaking his head.

I did not know when the words escaped my lips, 'You are an idiot too, Capo!' I said. He must have been surprised to hear that I could still babble as he walked closer and stared into my face. Then, came laughter, a mirthless howl that squeaked out of a graveyard.

'The idiot is babbling! The idiot is babbling! This idiot is still babbling!' He saying when Eliza emerged from her hut with a hilarious cry. 'Mama Aondo-a-k-a-a wam-o! Mama Aondo-a-k-a-a wam-o! Mama Aondo-a-k-a-a wam-o!' The woman was wailing with her arms wrapped around her head.

I heard an explosion from the pistol. Although, it appeared to me the bullet had missed Eliza, she went down and lay still. Her boy came and held her hand shaking her vigorously, crying 'Mammy… Mammy… Mammy…'

Tears began to roll down my cheeks too. I was touched to see the boy sit there and cry by his mother. Why was everything happening so fast? Why?

My heart bled for the boy, but I could not stop weeping for my mother also.

Capo and his group hurried back into the car. The engine of the Mercedes car came alive. It drove toward me, whirled around for a while and dusted the air. When the dust settled, the car was gone.

Neighbours began to come into the compound. Soon a crowd had gathered us.

A neighbour came and lifted me up to rest against the cashew trunk. My arm was hurt, shattered by the bullet. The crowd had grown fully. Adu knelt there by his mother, weeping and calling, 'Mummy, mummy…' He was still shaking her left arm when Mama's friend whom I had seen breaking firewood the day I arrived home rushed into the compound, throwing her hands in the air and wailing. She ran across the compound towards Mama's corpse where it lay in the sun beside the bundle of firewood and the basket. Someone else ran into the compound; a man who worked at the Health Care Center. He ran to Mama's body and sitting by it he bent on and placed his ear on the chest. He must have checked if she was still alive. Then he shook his head in agony. He left for Eliza, pushed Adu aside, and began the same test he did on Mama. He placed his hands on the chest and pumped cautiously. Eliza coughed and opened her eyes dully.

It was one month after Mama had been buried. Eliza had fully recovered after she was hospitalized at the clinic for nearly a week. Father Gregory invited me to his sitting room for a discuss. When I came and sat, he started by telling me that he had written a letter to the Bishop in Makurdi requesting for an additional priest to be posted in to help him concentrate on the church in Akan. The other priest would go around the clans to do the pastoral work. 'I feel guilty that my continuous absence in the church allowed a number of recent happenings', he apologized.

'Whatsoever went wrong was not your fault Father- but it is good to have another priest come in to give a supporting hand', I replied.

The aged priest took a deep breath. 'Jesus Christ said: "Come unto me all you that labour and are heavy laden, and I will give you rest." He coughed, apologized, stretched his hand and made for the Bible which was on a table beside his chair. He opened the Bible and read from it, '...and this same Jesus was lifted up for our transgressions.' He closed the book and turned to me, 'My son, Jesus has thought us to be strong in all situations. God is faithful to comfort us and give us a new beginning, if we only come to Him and surrender our all; if we only recognize how worthless our efforts are without Him; if we can but plead with Him to take over our lives.'

My hand, which was still healing, ached a bit. I supported it on to the arm of the chair as the priest continued, 'God is always knocking on the door of our hearts!' With that, the priest smiled.

'It is written that man has sinned and that is why Jesus is made manifest to us. Jesus is manifested as the fountain of life to whosoever thirsts. But Son, you really have to understand this that God has forgiven you. You have to understand it deeply, in fact that you must also forgive yourself to move on in life. Self-forgiveness permutes a man's true strength. You see, it is written that God gave Jesus Christ a name above all names. I will tell you what this means. Humankind is sinful, fallible, and weak. All of us are weak and sinful before God, and even before fellow humans! But when we fall, and in our failure we recognize and call on God through Jesus, we remind God of His Love. And he will always hear us. Always.' The man paused.

I had heard those words several times before that day. But when I heard them at that moment, they meant much more to me.

'Can you let God take off your burden, son?' Father Gregory asked.

I nodded slowly.

'Can you let Jesus in and let your pains out?'

'Father, I will.'

The priest drew closer now and held me by the hand and asked, 'In your confession yesterday you said you had carnal knowledge of a girl in your school?' I nodded. 'You said her cult brother came here and killed your mother?' I nodded. 'Nothing is too much for God to forgive,' the priest said then began to pray for me. When he was done with the prayer, he asked, 'Now, are you willing to go back to school to continue with your education?'

It was a heavy question to answer. How could I go back to that graveyard called a university, where are goodness had died and campus cultism was fast growing as a replacement?

After a while, I answered, 'Yes, I will go back to school Fada'.

Mama had always wanted me to be educated. Now, her wish had become even more pertinent to me. And I was going back to school to excel, to make her proud even if she was no more physically present here on earth with me.

'Aondodukarr, when you return to school, you will have to let go of this girl.'

'Yes Father, I will,' I said.


**II**

Will I ever forgive Joe? Will I ever forgive that boy who calls himself Capo? Will I ever get along well with Anita again?

I have learnt thus far to be kind to friends. I know that a friend can push one up, pull down, hold stagnant, build or destroy. I have learnt how to choose my friends. But heck! Though the herd is at all times wrong, if it pays, there's nothing erroneous with being a sheep. Who was it that once said such strong words? Sometimes, it is best to just wonder.

## Glossary

**Ajuju:** The male sex organ, especially a boy's.

**Ankara:** A native fabric.

**Danshiki:** An armless garment for men and women, mostly used in West Africa.

**Fiaaaa:** Quickly.

**Fiap:** Done quickly, with no delay

**Ghana-must-go**: A polythene bag used in Nigeria.

**Koboko:** A whip.

**Kpash:** To exclaim in surprise.

**Luaegh:** The teak tree.

**Luam:** Yam paste made by pounding well cooked peeled yams in a mortar.

**Nune:** Local seasoning.

**Nyash:** The buttocks or anus.

**Oga:** Senior or boss; used to show respect to someone in a position of authority.

**Oyibo:** A non-black person, especially those white.

**Pikin:** Of a child, especially a boy.

**Sojas:** A corrupt way of pronouncing 'Soldier'

**Toho-gile:** Elephant grass.

**Ugwu:** Pumpkin leaf.

www.ingramcontent.com/pod-product-compliance
Lightning Source LLC
Chambersburg PA
CBHW030327160726
47992CB00005B/2187